Dedicated to my good friends
A big thanks to my family – thank

Most of all a big thanks to my readers, I hope you continue to enjoy my work for many years to come.

And a shout out for the Ely Writers Group – hopefully I'll see you Wednesday!

Keep up with my latest news and releases via my blog:
http://thecultofme.blogspot.co.uk/

You can also follow me on Twitter:
http://www.twitter.com/TheCultofMe

Editing by Alex Roddie from Pinnacle Editorial:
http://www.pinnacleeditorial.co.uk/

Cover image provided by Magic Owl Design
http://www.magicowldesign.com/

© 2015 Michael Brookes - All rights reserved

OTHER BOOKS BT MICHAEL BROOKES

The Third Path Trilogy

The Cult of Me
Conversations in the Abyss
The Last True Demon

Morton & Mitchell Series

Faust 2.0

Other

Sun Dragon
Elite: Legacy
An Odd Quartet
An Odder Quintet

Chapter 1
Finding the Impossible

The Garden of Eden had seen better days.

Where a paradise once existed now I saw a churned battlefield, reminiscent of the blood-soaked fields of France during World War I. Unlike the tragedy of the human conflict, this war had raged for longer than the span of human existence. In the process the war ruined the splendour of the Garden which had once been the jewel of creation. Hemal, the Friar and Hammond waited for me to act; fortunately the sheer scale of Eden enabled us to appear far from the current fighting.

Or so I hoped at any rate.

During my incarceration within the monastery wall, the conversations with the angels provided me with some warning of what to expect. Despite that I still felt somewhat shell-shocked by the experience. The transformation from a living human into an immortal soul wasn't an easy or pleasant one.

The Friar and Hammond suffered an even greater trauma. Both refused to speak, or even acknowledge my presence. They retained the same physical appearance as they had in life. I assumed that I had too. The Friar was the taller of the two, although not by much. Hammond, the ex-marine bulked much heavier.

I'd first met them both in prison. Hammond had been one of the guards and the Friar replaced the chaplain I'd scared away. Unbeknownst to me at the time they were both members of the Dominican order and my particular talents were of great interest to them.

They had talents of their own of course, but they relied upon their framework of faith. I preferred to be more flexible and that helped me through the transition between life and death. I'd also received some warning of what the process entailed, they found everything they believed in life ruined like the Garden around them. Only the angel Hemal seemed aware of my presence and she looked almost dead from her battle with that traitorous bastard Venet.

When I last encountered him he'd distracted me while the Antichrist prepared for my sacrifice. The moment when he'd torn Lazarus' miracle of immortality from my body had been one of infinite agony. In the same moment I had died — something I'd thought impossible after stealing the miracle from Lazarus.

I'd learnt that we all possessed an immortal soul. A construct created by God which existed in planes of being higher than our own. It followed us throughout our lives recording our choices and thoughts. When we died it transformed our consciousness into a new being able to inhabit the same plane as the angels.

Sounds great, doesn't it?

Like all pleasant-sounding things, it came with a catch. In the instant of transformation you experienced every living second of your life. More than just memories, you also discovered every truth about yourself and what you might have been. Every choice you ever made was laid bare and the consequences of your actions, or failure to act, made clear.

In effect you didn't just relive the life you had; you followed every life you could have led. Imagine all the ways in which your life might have differed. Now live them all at once in the same instant. It created an information overload even for someone used to walking the paths of the mind like me.

I knew what to expect and still struggled to comprehend the experience. Hammond and Friar Francis looked like they had been fried by theirs.

From far in the distance came the sound of conflict. The eternal war had already lasted longer than the universe. A few thousand years ago humanity joined the war as cannon fodder for both sides, the loyalists and the fallen. One of the loyalists sat in front of me now. Lucifer and Michael had put a plan in action to end humanity's existence and our involvement in the war.

When I first met Hemal I'd almost been seduced by her ethereal beauty. That fair art had been ruined by Venet. She had suffered so much damage I caught glimpses of her true form boiling beneath the human-shaped disguise she wore for our benefit.

She'd once warned me that seeing her true form would be too much for my mind to handle. I wondered if that still held true, or if the transformation somehow protected me. I guessed it would. After all, if it didn't then the growing rebellion from the human souls would have been crushed by now.

Her true form reminded me of the coiling mass which once protected Lazarus's mind. No, at first glance it might have seemed similar, but upon closer inspection they stretched deeper. I followed the twists inwards ...

"Hey! You can admire me later when I'm back to my usual self."

Her words brought me back. I didn't understand why I'd lost myself so easily. Something with my mind didn't seem right; my usual precision had somehow slid off-kilter.

I glanced again at the Friar and Hammond. They looked the same as they had back in the physical universe. Again my concentration slipped — why was I so easily distracted all of a sudden?

Another memory intruded. Something more recent.

"You said that we still had a chance to stop Lucifer and Michael's plan. You said we needed to find the last true demon. I thought you'd hunted them all down?"

This was one of the secrets I'd learned while in my cafe beside the abyss: demons weren't part of creation. Somehow they were invisible to God. This had frightened the angels and they'd hunted down and destroyed all of them.

Or so they'd claimed.

"That's what we thought, but I've heard rumours over the centuries." Her voice strained from the effort of talking. "Strange occurrences which might indicate one still exists."

"How is this possible?"

"I'm not sure, and we don't have time to speak of this now. Others will have sensed your arrival and you're still a valuable prize. We must get out of here and quickly."

"Where to?"

"Anywhere for now. I'm too weak to fight even a human soul in my current condition."

"All right, let me get Hammond and Friar Francis together."

She nodded.

I moved over to the Friar and looked into his eyes. He didn't respond to my presence. I saw nothing in his eyes, just a stare which reached out forever.

"Friar, we have to move. I realise this is all seems strange and isn't what you expected, but Hemal says we cannot stay here."

Still no sign of life. I touched his arm. I'm not one for physical contact. I much prefer to delve into people's thoughts, but I hoped it would get through to him — a silly idea I know, but I'd experienced all manner of odd notions since I first met these two men.

Again my mind wandered so I forced my focus back to the Friar.

"C'mon Friar, we need to get out of here. Snap out of it."

Still no response. I tried shaking him but, once again, nothing. I only had one choice left, so I cast out my thoughts and dived into his mind.

Well that had been the plan; instead nothing happened. The first time we'd met his abilities had blocked my own, but this was something worse — my will didn't even leave my head. For the first time since an early age I couldn't project my will beyond my own body.

I tried again with the same result.

I didn't panic until my third attempt failed. I grabbed the Friar again, this time with creeping desperation and hoping physical contact would provide a bridge. When it didn't I really started to fear. I released the Friar and turned to Hammond.

The Friar had blocked me before, although since training me he hadn't been able to do that. A small part of me had already understood that I wasn't being blocked, not by the Friar. The greater and weaker part needed even the flimsiest of straws to clutch at.

I tried to cast my mind out once more.

It failed to leave the prison of my skull. Hammond didn't even look at me. He'd always been so secure in himself that he never raised any barriers; in fact he'd welcomed me straight in the first time we'd met. Now he stared past me, not registering my panic or even the wreckage of the Garden around him.

In that moment I experienced fear. Not for the first time I'll grant you, but this time proved different. This wasn't as simple as a fear of dying, or being beaten. This fear struck at the core of who I had been for so long. I reacted as I had before and retreated inside myself.

The relief when I slipped into the fabric of my own mind thrilled me. Was it really still my body even though I no longer had a physical body?

It was a distracting question and not one I should take the time to dwell on. I faced an existential concern: something which had defined me for most of my life had vanished. I felt lessened by the knowledge.

Deep inside I discovered a small sanctuary. It buoyed me that at least I had a place to retreat to. The knowledge restored my faith in myself. Not completely of course but enough to keep me retreating into the same state that Hammond and the Friar already had.

Chapter 2
Sky Full of Trouble

A scream shattered creation.

The shock of it dragged me from the comfort of my own mind and sparked a fresh fear. What the hell was going on? So far I had a handle on what was happening to us, but this was new. Hemal also flinched from the terrible noise.

Hammond and the Friar remained undisturbed, which puzzled me more than the ground-shaking vibrations. How could they not hear it? Were they so far apart from what happened around them? If so, how would I bring them back?

The sound faded.

The moment after filled with a portent of dread and my fear deepened.

I didn't usually surrender to fear. Don't get me wrong, I didn't pretend it didn't exist, but back in my life I rarely encountered anything worthy of the emotion. I'd been in the Garden for only a few minutes and already I'd been in fear of something for most of it.

Hemal looked at me and I recognised the same emotion on her face as well.

That didn't help my nerves at all.

She opened her mouth to speak and a second scream drowned her out. I wouldn't have considered it possible, yet it sounded louder than the first. The concussion of it pounded against me, knocking me to the ground.

I lay flat on my back as the scream pummelled my senses. Amidst the confusion I smelled something odd: the scent of ozone, familiar from my time living on the streets. A storm approached.

The memory tricked me. This wouldn't be a thunderstorm. I sensed something far more sinister in the air but lacked any comprehension of what it might be. Not then, but I would learn soon enough.

A wound appeared in the sky — a line so small I didn't notice it at first. With the overwhelming cacophony that was hardly a surprise. The pressure of the assault convinced me that retreat would be a wise move. I doubted I would escape the noise completely, but at least I could mount some form of defence.

The cool depths of my mind beckoned but as I withdrew a blemish in the sky caught my attention. What looked like a shadow at first lengthened into a tear. Through it I saw darkness. Something primal insisted that here was an event I needed to witness.

It widened further still, each movement accompanied by a fresh scream. I fancied I saw a lone star in the black and it winked at me.

The screams now overlapped each other and crashed down upon us. Even the Friar and Hammond had been forced to the ground, although they showed no other sign of being aware of events around them.

With one final shriek the tear opened to fill the sky and through it I saw something which filled me with dread and wonder. I saw the blue globe so familiar to its inhabitants. Clouds twisted across the oceans and curled in storms covering most of the surface.

The Earth moved towards the tear in the sky. As wide as the gap looked, the globe stretched it further as it pushed its way through. We witnessed creation giving birth to the world and it screamed with the overwhelming agony of it. The tear snapped closed behind as the world squeezed from the physical universe and into the sky above Eden.

After the sky slammed shut the tone of the sound changed; it became more complicated. Within the scream of the world, choirs of smaller voices combined in an unending chorus of suffering.

Seven billion voices all cried out to the perfect sky as they died in the same instant. I sensed their deaths in more ways than my hearing. Even though I now lacked the ability to reach out with my mind, the shockwave of so many deaths smashed through us all.

Pain from the vibrations convulsed me. My glance swept across our small group and for a moment I thought I saw something flicker across the Friar's face. Hope bloomed; I needed his sensible support right now. The tsunami of death shredded my senses, and my sudden deficiency threatened a greater despondency within me.

The hope was snatched away a second later as the Friar's expression returned to its previous blank state. His body convulsed in the same pattern as mine, but no sign of discomfort, —or anything at all — showed on his face.

For several minutes the noise continued and when it stopped I didn't notice for quite some time. The echo of it rang through my body with a violence even I couldn't assimilate. Stunned, I stared at the planet as it floated in the sky.

One of my favourite dreams was to journey into orbit. I didn't want to become an astronaut; no, I just wanted to see space unmarred by the atmosphere and to see the Earth as I did now. I remembered an astronaut saying how she'd considered the view of Earth must have been like looking down from Heaven.

How little she understood.

In that short moment of clarity I regretted how narrow my focus had been. With my ability I could have fulfilled my dream, but now it was too late.

Strange for me to experience regret, even in such a transitory way.

Too late as well to find the last true demon mentioned by Hemal. Lucifer and Michael's plan had succeeded. The Garden would soon be filled with the entire human race — fresh food for the two armies and once they'd crushed their common foe they would resume their eternal war.

It occurred to me that they didn't want their war to end, then I remembered Venet's revelation. Lucifer certainly wanted to end the war, but only in his favour. The power of self in action I supposed.

I then considered whether I would have to find the demon. If anything could stir God from his contemplation then surely the complete annihilation of our race would do the trick. He'd created the Garden of Eden specifically to welcome human souls after their transformation.

There had to be meaning there somewhere.

A foolish hope.

Only then did I realise the noise had stopped. Instead a silence pregnant with doom rested upon us. Hemal looked at me and started to speak, but as she did so a new sound drowned out her words.

This noise sounded pure as the toll of a bell. It resonated through everything. It didn't cause any pain this time, just a cold vibration and a deepening in the pit where my stomach had once resided.

Yet I sensed this would be something worse.

The tremors had ceased and I carefully stood up; it felt good to be upright. Silly I know, but it didn't sit well with me to be cowering and lying defeated on the floor.

My earlier fear proved correct. As I looked up at our planet, something terrible occurred and all I could do was watch as the destruction unfolded

Antarctica unpeeled in a ragged ribbon.

An entire continent was torn away from the globe like the peel of an orange. Another shriek shattered the sky as the atmosphere whipped away in a single gust.

The world's oceans crashed down upon the Garden in a deluge not witnessed since the great flood. I gave thanks to a God who I knew existed — but didn't listen — that we weren't underneath the downpour. In the distance I watched a great wave from the sea falling from the sky.

Powerless I looked up and saw the land continued to peel away, forming a disk of pulverised matter suspended in the firmament.

For a few seconds a glowing globe of molten rock and lava hung in the sky and then fell towards the ground.

Chapter 3
Underground

A column of fire plunged from the sky and struck the fallen oceans with a titanic hiss of steam. The molten guts of the Earth fell to the Garden, vaporising the water and smothering the ground. The liquid rock formed a new tidal wave and chased after the smaller one of water. This vast wall of burning rock moved slower than the one of water, but both sped in every direction.

The Earth's crust hung above the falling lava. That too would fall and when it did the shock waves would wreak terrible destruction upon Eden.

We needed to find shelter, but I had no idea where.

Hemal arrived at the same conclusion.

"We can hide in the tunnels."

"What tunnels?"

"They were created by human souls seeking refuge from the angelic hunting parties. From both sides."

It didn't matter where the tunnels originated, just that we had some way to escape the incoming end.

"Where are these tunnels?"

"They stretch underneath most of Eden."

"How do we get to them?"

"I'll have to create an entrance, but it won't be easy. It will take all my strength and we don't have much time. As soon as the way opens get inside."

I looked at Hammond and the Friar.

"How will we get them in?"

"You'll have to find a way. Drag them if you have to, but be quick; we have a few minutes at best."

Hemal closed her eyes and a new shaking started near me. I heard a sudden pop and a hole appeared in the ground. Looking into its maw, I saw a tunnel stretched into the depths. Its side looked smooth like plastic.

"You need to hurry!"

She sounded so weak, and for a second indecision froze me by the entrance. Who should I move first? Hammond's bulk would make him the most difficult to move, so I chose him first.

He didn't respond when I grabbed him and started pulling him to the tunnel. I only had to drag him several yards, but he weighed more than I did and, while he didn't resist, he didn't aid me either. I shouted at him as I moved, trying to wake him so he could help.

It took all my strength to pull him to the tunnel. All the while the approaching roar gained in volume and the ground's shaking made movement more difficult.

Friar Francis was almost as tall as Hammond, but much slighter of build so I moved him more easily. A fresh tremor more violent than any so far knocked me from my feet. I tried again and this time I felt him twitch and dropped him in surprise.

"Friar?"

He looked up at me, his expression still confused.

"What's happening?" he asked.

"There's no time. We have to get in the tunnel."

"Hurry!" Hemal urged.

I didn't need telling, I understood what approached, but I couldn't get up again. Every time I tried the ground shook and knocked me back down. Each attempt chewed up valuable seconds. I cursed loudly, my voice weak against the rushing wave. "You must get into the tunnel. Now, I will close it behind you."

Scrambling clumsily across the trembling ground we ignored Hemal's instruction and crawled to her. The sound of an express train charging at us drowned out her further demands to leave her behind. We understood how little time we had, but the Friar wanted to save her. My motives were less pure; she knew this world we now inhabited, and we needed her to guide us.

Together we dragged her towards the tunnel. The roar around us grew louder. It now deafened us and the changes in pressure made it difficult to breathe.

A part of my mind wondered why. Surely souls didn't need to breathe? Perhaps our minds became so engrained with the body's needs after a lifetime of use that they continued to go through the familiar motions.

The ground now trembled so violently that we saw the surface pulsating with the pressure. The movement made even crawling difficult, especially dragging Hemal's dead weight. The sound roared so loud it hurt to hear and we all screamed in counterpoint.

The tunnel entrance looked so close. We only had a few more yards to go, but movement became impossible. I shouted back in fury, my voice lost in the approaching storm. I had never felt so helpless. I didn't know what a wave of water followed by molten rock would do to my already dead soul. I suspected I would survive, but that I wouldn't enjoy the experience.

We tried. We pushed ourselves with all our might to cross those final yards. I even tried to move forward without pulling Hemal as well, but still the pulsating ground pushed us back.

Then a moment of calm.

The sound around me ceased. I saw the Friar's lips moving, but I couldn't make out what he said. The silence seemed false, like the pause between two moments.

More significantly the ripples ceased.

That gave us the chance we needed. We took the opportunity and in a single dash escaped into the tunnel, all three of us falling down the incline onto Hammond who remained unresponsive.

Hemal groaned with the effort, but closed the tunnel and sealed us in darkness as the world rained down upon us.

Chapter 4
Slam Dunk

The wave of water struck first. It echoed in the tunnel with a dull roar. At first I feared it would soak through the ground and into the tunnel, but the arrival of the larger wave of lava dispelled that fear and took the trouble to deliver a new one.

Even through the walls we heard the water vaporise as the burning rock drowned the flood. The hiss of steam sounded like the biggest steam engine ever created. The sound didn't last long, but the wave of rock did and continued for what seemed like hours. Above ground the sound had shocked us with its violence; down here it was an order of magnitude worse.

The grinding and smashing from the walls suppressed any chance of conversation. The walls emitted a faint glow, enough so we made out the shapes of each other. The wall felt smooth to the touch, like glass. I wondered how they had been made.

"They are formed from human souls." Hemal's voice entered my mind and interrupted my musings. Now she mentioned it, there was something familiar when I touched the slick surface.

"Unlike angels your kind cannot create or change creation directly."

I remembered Venet telling me of how the angels had created Heaven and later Hell, but God created the environment in which they were built. In fact they crafted their realms from the fabric of his mind.

A glimpse of something flashed before me, but escaped before I could grasp it. A new level of agony lanced through my ears. The Friar cried out. I didn't hear him, but I did see him crumple and hold his head in his hands. Even the statuesque Hammond showed signs of distress.

The wall against my back now burned my flesh; a pulse of colour, red as blood, shimmered across the walls.

"We must move!"

The glowing walls cracked into a network of dull red veins. I grabbed Hammond and pulled him along the tunnel. Friar Francis did the same with Hemal.

We withdrew deeper into the passagways as fresh fractures splintered the walls around us. Another impact shook the tunnel; we kept retreating. A third impact, greater this time, knocked us to the ground and destroyed the soul binding the tunnel together.

It collapsed and so did we with exhaustion.

I felt weakened, but still tried to cast out to Hemal. I hadn't accepted that the loss of my projection ability could be permanent and I wanted to understand more about how people built the tunnel from themselves. I also wanted to decide what we would do next. More shakes indicated impacts somewhere close, although the wall next to me remained cool.

All of us looked drained of vitality, except for Hammond who just lay where he'd fallen, staring beyond the wall. I wondered what, if anything, had caught his attention.

I withdrew inside myself again and examined the lucid moment we'd experienced before our escape in the tunnel. I was glad the Friar had recovered his senses and it made me wonder if that had something to do with the strange moment.

As I recalled the event the memory wrapped around me. It didn't feel like I observed a memory; it felt more like world around me warped into the reality of what happened rather than the moment I currently existed in.

The sensation disorientated me. I felt divided as if in two places at once. No, that wasn't right — as if I existed in two times at once. That made no sense.

I drifted with these thoughts, teasing at them, trying to make sense of the weird situation. Nothing in my experience compared to this. My thoughts followed different trails in a multitude of directions.

All of them at once.

Even stranger than that, I comprehended them.

Well, for a short time anyway.

Three seconds to be exact.

For those three seconds I experienced another period of lucidity, but it overwhelmed me. I vomited. Not quite, but my body went through the motions. I dry heaved for a while and allowed that to soak up my focus. It hurt, but still better than the horrible split moment.

Even worse — I couldn't say why.

It wasn't fear, exactly, or confusion. The perfect clarity threatened to obliterate me, to make me everything where I only wanted to be me.

It just didn't make sense.

I returned to the Garden and the tremors from the aftershocks of the impacts. They lasted for hours, but at least the noise abated somewhat now we'd moved deeper into the tunnels.

And so we waited.

Chapter 5
Deep Inside

The tremors lasted for hours. When the glow flickered, we moved deeper into the tunnel in case another collapse occurred. I tried to resume the mental conversation with Hemal, but once again I failed to cast outside myself and she appeared to be growing weaker with each passing minute.

When the rumbling stopped I caught the Friar's attention and we both moved over to her.

"We need to help her," I told him.

The Friar nodded in reply. We both knew what to do and laid our hands upon her arms. Her skin felt cold and alien to the touch.

The continuous rumbling from the impacts and the aftershocks had frayed our nerves, but we concentrated inward and then released our will to Hemal.

I shouldn't have been surprised. Again my will failed to leave my mind. My own form created a barrier for my abilities.

The Friar enjoyed more success, enough to give her the strength to open her eyes.

"Why don't my powers work?" I asked her.

At least I had my priorities right.

She shook her head. I looked at the Friar; he shrugged.

"I don't know." Hemal's voice sounded paper-thin.

I tried again. I sensed my power. It still resided within me, but it wouldn't release. I wanted to heal Hemal as well. It didn't sit well with me seeing her wounded, but I had to know. More than that I didn't know what might be looking for us and while the tunnel had saved us from the destruction of Earth I didn't feel secure there.

"What changed me in the transformation?"

I tried to determine if there had been some other cause. The transformation was the only change I was aware of — or rather the only thing that might have changed me in this way.

"I have no idea!" the Friar snapped. "I don't know what happens during the change. I'm still trying to understand it myself!"

"Why can you still project your will?"

"I don't know!"

I'd never seen the Friar exasperated before. He always appeared so calm under pressure. This all had to be strange for him too; after all, the same transformation had caused Hammond to retreat from the world.

Knowing that didn't help my current predicament. The only person who might be able to tell me anything was the angel who had passed out again. I hoped she knew something — that she could provide some clue as to why my abilities now failed me. Perhaps I could find out for myself, and I recalled my time with the Friar when we'd first met.

Well, not when we'd first met, more like some time later after I'd accepted my fate — or pretended to. I needed to approach this in the same way I'd approached the exercises he'd set me.

"All right, let's work this through," I told him. "Can you see inside my head?"

He focused for a few seconds.

"No. I couldn't after you'd mastered shielding anyway, but there isn't a barrier blocking me — at least not like any I've seen before. It's solid. Do we have time for this?"

"At the moment I'm useless. I need to understand."

"There are no imperfections, no space at all."

Learning that had been my first lesson from the Friar: nothing is completely solid. There's always a space in between, you just had to find it.

"How is that possible?"

"I don't know — it shouldn't be, but I suppose things work differently here."

"But you were able to cast your will out?"

"Yes."

Ok, so the Friar wasn't affected in the same way and that told me something. I didn't understand what it meant, but at least I'd learned something I didn't know a minute ago.

"All right." I pondered for a moment and then asked: "Can you enter Hammond's mind?"

Again I watched as he concentrated. He grimaced at what he found there.

"It's as open as he's always been, but there's something very wrong in there. I've never seen a mind so desolate."

Hammond had always been so strong, a man of faith and integrity. My polar opposite you might say.

Was that still true?

Perhaps not. Even so, it didn't help solve the pressing issue.

"Stay with me, Friar. We'll help Hammond, but we need to find a way for me to use my will. Try entering Hemal's mind."

A look of wonder wiped away the grimace.

"My God, this isn't a mind — this is the universe. I've never seen anything so magnificent."

I understood his sense of amazement. I'd experienced the same myself when first trying to enter an angel's mind. The sheer complexity and scale of it astonished me. From what I remembered her mind spanned greater than any universe.

"Come back, Friar. You can't get lost in there; we need you here."

He didn't respond at first and I worried that he'd lose himself and drift in the expanse of the angel's psyche.

"Wait, she's trying to tell me something." He nodded with understanding to a voice I couldn't hear. "We can help her. If we can wake her then she can use our strength to heal herself."

"Can she access my will even with whatever is blocking me?"

"She thinks so."

I didn't like the idea of my abilities being a one-way street, but we needed Hemal conscious. Without her knowledge we were lost and I knew all too well that powerful entities stalked the ruins of the Garden: more powerful than us, especially with me in a crippled state.

"Ok then, how do we wake her?"

"The same way I did before, but there's a problem."

Of course there was.

"Two of us aren't enough to heal her," the Friar continued. "It would drain us too much. We need Hammond as well."

"No problem. We can drag him over."

"That won't work; he has to grant her his essence. It'll only work if we can bring him back to his senses."

"How can we do that?"

"You have to find him."

"Find him how?"

"The same way you found Lazarus: you'll need to go into his mind and find him and restore him."

"I can't leave my own body. How can I enter his mind?"

The Friar looked troubled.

"Well?"

"She said that if you can't go outwards then there's only one other way to go."

"What the hell is that supposed to mean?"

"She must mean go inwards. That's how you started, wasn't it?"

I nodded. It was true. I had a knack for looking inward, but how would that enable me to connect with Hammond?

"Is that all she has to say?"

"I'm afraid so; she's very weak. It's up to us now."

"All right. You see if you can get through to Hammond by conventional means. I'll see about looking inward, although I have no idea what I'm looking for."

"There'll be some connection."

"Like what?"

"I don't know — see what you can find."

Chapter 6
Downward Spiral

We moved Hammond over and placed him beside Hemal. His face remained blank and, as before, he didn't respond to our presence. The glow of the walls meant we could see for a hundred yards in both directions. Where we had come from was blocked by the collapse. What lay in the other direction we had no idea.

The Friar crouched beside Hammond, holding the big man's hand and murmuring words of comfort and support. They went unheard.

I caught myself drifting again.

I commanded myself to focus. Even in my days of drug exploration my will had been more reliable than this. Perhaps it was connected in some way to whatever sealed me within my own body.

In fairness I should have been used to the experience by now. When sealed within the monastery walls I had been locked within my flesh without any avenue for escape. Then I had retreated deep within myself to the abyss — the place within us all where the veil between our world and the next resides.

I had found refuge there, but would I also find answers?

I doubted it.

For some reason I hesitated. I decided to try and apply reason to the situation. I'd come to rely on my gifts over the years. What if they failed me again when I tried to delve inward?

I didn't think the barrier was a normal part of the process. If that was true then why could the Friar still project his will? No, after some consideration I believed it to be a deliberate act; someone had done this to me. An even scarier thought occurred. What if I had done it to myself?

I didn't like that thought, but it did interest me.

If the block could be dealt with from the inside then perhaps I had done it to myself. Was that what Hemal had hinted at?

More to the point, why would I do such a thing and why didn't I know for sure if I had done this to myself? Blaming someone seemed more plausible and also more acceptable to me, or at least to my ego.

A stray musing returned me to the moment of transformation. It had taken an instant, yet stretched for eternity.

The thought led me to the lucid moment before the tunnel, when all had seemed lost. Were these things all connected? If so, how?

I reached inside myself for the memory and discovered something odd. The tableau existed there in the timeline of my memories, but not in a pattern I recognised. My other memories existed as they always had — coherent fragments of senses and feelings.

With some effort they became malleable, but in changing them they turned unreal, fictions of my imagination. This memory seemed different. I poked at it and it refused to bend. The sequence remained untouched no matter what I did to it.

Another difference proved to be one of perspective. In my regular memories the perspective was always mine, but I could manipulate it, view it from other angles. With this memory it was different. My perspective encompassed the whole scene simultaneously.

I delved deeper into the moment, playing it back and forth like a movie in the ultimate 3D, examining it from every angle and searching for some weakness.

From this wider perspective I saw the ruin of the world, things I could not have seen. Did I imagine this? I used to be an acolyte of psychedelics; I loved the trips, visual and otherwise. From them I'd learned the art of discerning hallucinations from reality. This was no illusion.

Although isn't truth simply a matter of perspective?

My mind wandered again and this time I believed I understood why. I was trying to focus on too much and that overwhelmed my thoughts and caused the distractions. My mind tried to focus on what it didn't understand.

I rewound the memory and watched the waves surge across the Garden. First the world's oceans swept the surface clean. Then the larger wave of lava followed in its wake. I wondered what had happened to the billions of souls fresh from Earth's destruction.

And you know what?

I wished I could have stopped it.

Back then I doubt I could have told you why, and I'm not sure I know now. Perhaps the Friar and Hammond had been a bad influence on me. On the other hand it might have been as simple as the fact that I liked the hunting. No more people meant no more lives to torment.

There's nothing quite like a bit of self-deception.

I returned to the focus on the memory, which took more effort than before, as if it resisted me. I accepted this as a good sign; it was trying to hide something from me. All I had to do was figure out its secret.

A memory that wasn't a memory, more like a slice of reality captured inside my head.

The truth is a matter of perspective.

I had to look inward.

My abilities worked within the confines of my mind.

I watched the scene replay.

Merging myself into the memory I cast my will into Hammond's mind and it flew straight in.

Chapter 7
Shattered Faith

How could I be certain this was really Hammond's mind and not a delusion created by my own? The truth is I couldn't. It felt real and I would never have imagined the inside of Hammond's mind looking anything like the desolation stretched out before me.

I'd first entered Hammond's mind back in the chapel of my first prison where I'd planned a bloodbath suitable to mark my passing. The openness of his mind surprised me. He was fully aware of my presence, but didn't mind one bit.

Never had I encountered anyone so open and I hadn't since. The Friar protected his mind well, as did the others of his order. Of course they're all dead now and I wondered if they were still able to protect themselves after they'd crossed over. They'd be thrown straight into a war they weren't prepared for and would need every possible advantage.

Even more than that — they'd discover the truth of what they'd believed in for all of their lives.

Drifting. Again.

Hammond's mind still lay open, all of his memories and desires moulded into a desolate landscape. Once it had been lush with life and promise, well-watered by a will safe in the knowledge he'd always done what was right.

At the centre of it all had stood a rock: a solitary monolith towering above all else. For a while I'd wondered what the rock had meant, its significance eluding me for quite some time. I finally realised that it represented his faith. His faith sustained him, had made him strong and now it had abandoned him.

The landscape of Hammond's mind had transformed into grey. I stooped to examine the dust covering everything, draining the colour from it all. I suspected this was all that remained of his faith. What had seemed unbreakable must have shattered during his soul's transition.

He had placed his faith in God, but more than that he had believed in something greater than himself. The universe was a shitty place; he did what he could to make it better. He strived to make it safer for those trapped in it. He believed in something beyond the world, a force of good which provided the impetus to keep trying to make the world a better place.

The truth didn't reveal what he had expected.

I'd always considered Hammond to be a practical man — he grounded his faith in the reality of the world. He'd seen many things, had experienced the darkness that humans are capable of sinking to. He hadn't expected God to be the fairy tale many believed, but he did believe that God provided a state of being to strive for.

His God had been someone who tested mankind severely, but ultimately cared. After death there would be a better place to go to, a place where everything would be made right.

Perhaps his faith had been a little idealistic after all, but what would I know? I'd always believed in nothing but myself, which hadn't worked out so well either. Still, it wasn't me locked in a catatonic state.

The truth proved to be so much harsher than his faith required. God indeed existed, but he didn't believe in Hammond. He didn't even comprehend that humanity existed in any practical sense. Even worse, there wasn't a better place — all he found was a battleground worse than any he'd experienced in the Middle East.

His faith had shattered with the truth and its detritus now lay in a fine powder over everything he had known in life.

I stood on the fringes of his mind and wondered what I should do next. The landscape provided no clue so I walked forward. Maybe I would find some hint at ground zero which would help me establish a connection.

My footsteps left imprints in the residue. Everything was silent. An oppressive heat swamped me, growing thicker as I moved forward. I remembered Lazarus using a similar (although somewhat more energetic) tactic when I invaded his mind. Did this mean Hammond was actively trying to stop me?

I hoped it did because if that were the case then at some level, deep down, he still functioned. At that point I feared that his mind had broken so completely there would be no way to restore him.

I took heart from another observation. The heat might have been uncomfortable, but it posed me no real danger. This contrasted with the more violent efforts Lazarus had wielded to try and evict me from his mind.

My plan had been simple — I just kept moving forward. The mind is a wondrous thing, but it is not boundless. It is centred on one thing, and that is the self. Somewhere in this grey desert lurked Hammond's true self, and he clearly didn't want to talk to me. If I found him then I hoped that I could figure out a way to get through to him.

The plan had worked with Lazarus; even in a drugged state he layered a range of defences. I wondered if Hammond would do the same.

There was only one way to find out.

I walked across the ashes of Hammond's faith, my footsteps quiet upon the dust. The heat increased the further I progressed. It soon became uncomfortable. I might have been in his mind, but I was also still within my own, so it required little effort to counter the heat with a localised cool breeze.

That gave me an idea; it seemed a good one at the time.

I gathered my will and created a vortex which sucked all of the dust from the landscape. Another impulse compressed the fragments into a rock. I tried to rebuild his faith, to force the reality of it back into his psyche.

A foolish idea, yet still I tried.

I pressed the dust together, crushing it into a tighter and tighter mass. It was just dust — it had no life of its own, and I found nothing of substance to bind together. Hammond's faith was a dead thing; there could be no simple resurrection here. I'd need more than will to fix what had broken.

Yeah, I don't why I thought that might work. Sometimes you just have to let the stupid ideas work their way out. I'm pleased to say that a more sensible idea bubbled to the surface in its wake.

After a while at any rate.

The more suitable idea came in the form of a question: where had Hammond's faith come from?

All around me were his thoughts, his dreams and his memories. Somewhere in here amongst his shattered history was the answer. I expanded my awareness, pushing it until it filled his mind. The mind is a miraculous treasure. When focused it can be smaller than an atom, but when it is open like Hammond's it becomes bigger than a universe.

Perhaps there hid a truth to be learned there.

I drifted through Hammond's memories, trawling through every event of his life seeking the clue I needed. What had sparked his faith? What had enabled his faith to build into the monolith I'd once seen?

A quote from a book I once read led me to his early childhood. I believe it was a Jesuit who said that if you gave him a child's mind then they would be God's forever. Maybe it wasn't a Jesuit, maybe it was a Dominican like the Friar; in the end I suppose it didn't really matter.

Hammond's childhood surprised me. I'd expected a rough background, the familiar story of poverty and its escape by joining the armed forces. Instead I saw a happy and comfortable childhood devoid of religion but filled with happiness.

In part his childhood reminded me of my own, the early parts of it anyway. I scrubbed forward looking for the change. There had to be one. He lived a normal childhood, studied hard at school, occasionally got into trouble, but nothing major.

It all looked normal.

I became captivated by the warmth of it; or rather I let the simple joy of it bring me back to my own memories. I found it hard to believe I once lived as a normal child — a fun time. I'd discovered my ability to invade and manipulate the minds of those around me. That had brought new pleasures into my life.

Adrift on my thoughts again, I steered my attention back to the matter at hand.

While I hunted through his memories I also looked for signs of his current self. Perhaps in the joy of his early memories he'd found his own Heaven and lost himself there. I hoped that wasn't the case, because if so, I'd have to tear it apart to free him.

Chapter 8
The Best of Memories

I followed the thread of Hammond's life. I watched as he left school and then went to college where, as well as his studies, he discovered drink and girls. He also discovered his size. A sudden growth spurt put him above his friends, not only in height but in bulk too.

His developed size attracted him to a new pastime: he joined the college rugby team and found that he enjoyed the rough contact of the sport. It also increased his drinking and attractiveness to girls, but nothing too extreme — he remained the well-balanced individual his upbringing had made him.

After college he went to university. In these memories I discovered the first turbulence of any note in his life. In the most classic of downfalls he met a girl, who became the light of his life and then destroyed it.

Marie was a troubled girl; he understood that on an intellectual level, if not an emotional one. The truth became all too clear on the dreadful day she jumped from a bridge onto the railway tracks below.

He should have known. The night he met her she'd attempted to kill herself. He'd noticed her in the pub, but for some reason had shied away from talking to her. He didn't usually lack confidence when talking with women. He wondered what that meant, but not at the time; that came later.

They exchanged the occasional glance throughout the evening. When he finally decided to go over he saw the table occupied by a middle-aged couple. He thought little of it until he later left the pub and, turning the corner into an alley for a shortcut, he discovered her lying on the ground.

The youthful Hammond assumed she'd passed out drunk so he checked to make sure she was ok. Only when he crouched beside her did he notice the blood from her slashed wrist. Their first night together was in a hospital where she remained unconscious until the next day while he sat beside her.

An event like that left an impression, especially inside an inexperienced and caring mind like Hammond's. I didn't judge Hammond's naiveté. I'd invaded a multitude of minds over the years and this wasn't the silliest circumstance I'd encountered. The young girl had been embarrassed when she awoke and saw Hammond sitting by her bed. She wanted her suffering to be private; it felt out of place for someone else to be there.

Hammond possessed a natural charm and the evening spent by her side had solidified the attraction he'd experienced in the bar. He deflected her demands for him to leave. Persistence reinforced his banter until he broke through her defences.

He didn't leave until he'd secured a promise from her to meet him again. She kept her promise and they met more and more. After a few weeks their new friendship turned romantic and unknown to him trouble fermented in her mind.

With the benefit of detachment I understood this hadn't been true love — whatever that might be — but for Hammond it might as well have been. His thoughts drifted to her whenever they were apart. When they were together he felt complete.

Seven months after they'd first met she killed herself.

That event triggered the change in his life.

He'd fallen apart with her death. The turmoil of his grief and confusion soaked his memories. On some level he realised from the first encounter that it had been a possibility but with the arrogance of youth he convinced himself that he could help her, to prevent her from carrying out the terrible act.

Even at an early age Hammond possessed the gift of reading people. The problem here was that his gift had been blinded by irrational hope — not to mention other more base emotions. Easy enough for me to judge as I dredged through his life, I guess, and no great surprise that his view of the world differed from mine.

He discovered more solace in drink than I had with the death of my mother, but only for a while. The love may have been a blend of infatuation and his need to help, but that didn't mean the grief wasn't genuine. It suppressed the guilt and loss for a short time. The time lasted long enough to wreck his studies. When he finally dragged himself back into the light of day he found it didn't matter, as he no longer desired to continue his degree.

Marie had lit a spark — a light now quenched, but also a guide for something. He emerged from the darkness with a desire to do something with the memory of the spark. He searched for a path, working with various charities. He helped wherever the opportunity arose yet still his life remained empty and unfulfilled.

A chance encounter (was there ever such a thing?) in a bar changed his path again. He signed up for the Royal Marines, in part to satisfy a buried desire for adventure, to see new sights, but also as another way to help those who suffered.

The marines proved a good choice for the lost Hammond. It restored discipline to his life and his physique and personality meant a natural fit. After some initial trouble settling in he breezed through basic training. He then deployed to foreign soil.

He first journeyed to Norway and endured the bitter cold as part of the Arctic warfare training cadre. He learned how to fight and survive in some of the hardest and coldest terrain on Earth. The training served him well on his next deployment to the Falkland Islands as part of the garrison standing by in case of another Argentinian invasion.

From the wet and cold of the South Atlantic he travelled to the blistering heat of the Middle East. Like many people before him he found God in the desert — not from a burning bush, or voices in his head, but instead from the prosaic source of the marine Chaplain stationed with them during his first tour in Afghanistan.

The action in that hot and war-torn country had been a contrasting confusion of fighting against the Taliban and hearts and minds operations with the locals. Often the enemy and those he helped appeared to be one and the same.

The conflict reflected Hammond's own inner turmoil. He enjoyed the action, the thrill and camaraderie of combat. He didn't take pleasure from killing, although at times he worried that he did. He also found balance and fulfilment in the civic aid programmes in the villages he protected.

During these visits he met the Chaplain. The Chaplain had earned the grudging respect of the village elders. This fascinated Hammond; their religions seemed very different, but their faith also looked exactly the same.

Hammond noticed something about the Chaplain that fascinated me as well. More than that I also recognised something familiar about him. He reminded me of the Friar; they possessed the same bearing, the same poise.

They also owned the same mind, or at least the surface of it. I guessed that they had probably received their mental training from the same people. Skipping ahead through Hammond's thoughts I learned the Chaplain had been ordained in the same order, although it had been the Friar years later than inducted Hammond into the Dominicans.

Once again I was amazed at the clarity of the memories. I experienced the reality of it in every detail. It might have been because these formed Hammond's reality, and I also wondered if changing his past would change his present — a crazy idea I'd readily admit, but I filed the idea away just in case my current plan didn't work out.

I rewound back to Hammond's first tour and the memories of constant dust and heat. Hammond had made himself at home in this harsh environment even though (or maybe because?) it was so different from the one he'd known back home.

In between patrols of sun-baked mountains and barely-irrigated fields Hammond talked with the Chaplain and entered a spiritual new world. The Chaplain guided his new pupil through this strange landscape beyond the physical and the intellectual.

Hammond cared little for the intricacies of theology, but the concept of a watching God, one who tested but ultimately cared for humanity, brought him some comfort. It made sense in a way that dispelled the darkness within him.

He had been saved.

His faith hadn't provided a quick fix, but in time it became a tower, built brick by brick — at first with the help of the Chaplain and later by his brethren, including the Friar. The process took many years, continuing for the rest of Hammond's life, right up until the point when he died and learned the truth.

Unfortunately for him, objective reality trumped personal belief. Transformation into a soul took the edge off his subjectivity.

That posed a problem for me. Hammond hadn't been born again. His faith hadn't started from mere rote learning either; instead it had formed from constant toil. It also meant his faith would need more than a quick and easy fix. It would have to be rebuilt over time. Time was something I didn't have.

I considered the idea I had earlier. Perhaps if I reconstructed his memories, in effect rebuilding his entire life, he would once again have something to believe in. For a second time I discarded the notion, this time because I didn't know what the effect would be. I didn't want to break Hammond — I needed him to be his usual self, and only with his full strength would he be useful.

My journey across his memories stopped; this wasn't working as it had with Lazarus. Lazarus had fought me at every step. Hammond still resisted, but not in any threatening way. No, he'd withdrawn into his mind, so deep that no trace of his self remained.

He'd retreated only once before in his life; then it was his belief in the world which had been shattered. Faith hadn't restored him then — rather it had been his basic nature of wanting to help, to balance the suffering he'd endured. His faith had come later.

I then understood what I needed to do. I couldn't rebuild his faith, but perhaps I could give him purpose again.

Chapter 9
Path to Salvation

Hammond's weakness (ok, some might call it strength) was that he cared. If he hadn't cared then the revelation wouldn't have broken him. I had to use his innate desire to help to bring him back.

Hemal had provided a slim chance of hope: if we located the last truc demon then maybe everything could be fixed. I struggled to pin my hopes on something so slim, but having something to focus on kept me going. With Hammond's help we would chase the dream, no matter how faint it might be. Without it we stood no chance at all.

I skimmed through his more recent memories to glean what he understood about our current situation. I found none. That made sense to me. If he understood the magnitude of the situation he wouldn't have withdrawn so deep.

That is what I hoped at any rate.

During my younger years the government of the time espoused the concept of the short, sharp shock. It was supposed to be a means to stop young hooligans becoming career criminals. It turned out to be not very successful, but I didn't want to change Hammond — I simply wanted to restore him.

I focused my will and transformed the terrain of his mind into the Garden of Eden, but not the Garden of his Bible; I presented the real Eden, the one ruined by the constant struggle between Heaven and Hell. I turned his mind into the moment before the Earth was pulled from the universe.

The final screams of seven billion souls filled his mind. I injected my memories of the end of humanity into the landscape of his inner self. It provided quite the spectacle; the sheer power of it amazed me. My recreation filled Hammond with every detail.

I stood surrounded by the maelstrom of the world's end. The rending of the tortured planet drowned out the screams of the souls wrenched without any warning from their lives. The world tore apart and rained fire upon Eden.

A shockwave struck my illusion. It wavered like a mirage and I smiled. Hammond had responded to the overwhelming horror which swamped his mind. He didn't want to experience what I — and the rest of humanity — had already suffered.

Not so long ago I would have been happy to torment another person with images of such torture; here I hesitated, but only for a moment. I had no choice. We needed Hammond to stand with us.

This might have been his mind, but despite his home advantage my will proved stronger. I strengthened the projection, pushing it deep into his being. The blazing fragments of the world smashed through his mind, each impact causing earthquakes which compounded the terrible noise.

Again the illusion shimmered as Hammond tried to banish it from his thoughts.

I forced my will into the re-enactment of those horrible events. Every part his mind now shuddered with the enormity of the world's end. As I continued to replay the events, the molten heart of the planet followed the deluge of the oceans.

Tremendous heat washed through his being and I detected a rumble. I sensed defiance — no not defiance, more like resistance. He wanted to deny the visions I forced him to endure. For them to be real would be horror beyond any he had experienced.

Unfortunately for Hammond I couldn't allow him the luxury of denying the reality of it. He had nowhere to retreat to so he tried to block the scene. His denials reverberated through the flood of steam and fire.

And then the world fell.

His mind shook with noise, pounding destruction as the world fell to ground and shattering Eden. I amplified the sound to beyond deafening levels; it hurt now to listen to the end. Mind quakes ravaged Hammond's thoughts.

"Stop."

I almost didn't hear his voice all alone in the storm.

He said it again and I stopped the devastation.

"Please stop."

His voice was a whisper, but without the destruction I heard him clearly.

"Hammond, you need to come back."

"I can't. There's nothing left."

"True, but we can fix that."

"How?"

"God can make it right."

He laughed although I heard more bitterness than joy in the sound. I chuckled too; that word didn't sound at all right coming from my lips.

"I once thought that, but now I know better."

"You really don't. It's not what you think."

"You've shown me that God has abandoned his children."

"It's more complicated than you realise; Hemal thinks she knows a way to make him realise what is happening."

He didn't know who Hemal was, of course; but meshed as our minds were in that moment he learned from my thoughts. Not that it seemed to matter.

"How can he not notice? The whole world has been destroyed."

"I realise this isn't what you expected."

"How can you understand? You have never believed. You have never devoted your life to something greater than yourself."

That was true. I believed in only one thing and that was myself. I'd always found life easier that way. It's true other people can help you — for example Hammond and the Friar had saved me more than once. On the flip side they'd bricked me inside a monastery wall as my reward for killing Lazarus for them.

Ok, so I had stolen Lazarus' miracle rather than follow orders and destroy it. Even so, it still seemed a little harsh.

The past didn't matter now. The world had changed since then and not for the better. I had played my part in those events; or rather I'd failed to stop them getting worse. While I tried to explain to Hammond why he should return to the land of the living (or what passed for it), I examined my own motivations. Contemplation comes naturally if you spend as much time in your own head as I had over the years.

I was pissed off to put it bluntly. I'd never taken defeat well and they don't come bigger than this one. I'd taken on the Antichrist — so sure of myself, lured by a prophecy claiming I was the one to save the world.

Not only had the Antichrist beaten me, he'd done so with contemptuous ease. The defeat had hurt almost as much as having the miracle torn from my flesh and that had been an agony beyond anything ever imagined. I wanted some payback for that — a petty consideration compared to the extinction of the human race and, don't get me wrong, I'd killed more than a few people in interesting ways, but total genocide requires a depth of evil even I didn't swim in.

I had no idea what would happen if by some small chance we managed to connect with God and restore everything, but even achieving that would be a win for my side and that suited me just fine. "Look Hammond, I appreciate this isn't what you'd expected."

"You got that right."

"But you've helped people throughout all your life, before you discovered religion. It's who you are. We have a comatose angel. The three of us can restore her and then we can right the wrong and bring humanity back. It's up to us."

He didn't answer right away, but I knew he was back. In truth I realised that when he'd appeared, talking was just a formality.

Hammond nodded.

"All right. What do we need to do?"

Chapter 10
Shriekers

We returned to the tunnel and its gloom. The Friar remained crouched by Hemal with a concerned look on his face. He turned as I groaned and moved, then exclaimed with joy to see his old friend returned to him. Hammond responded with a smile as they embraced.

"I'd say get a room," I told them and there might have been a shadow of jealousy in my voice. Their obvious bond forged through years of service together disturbed me. It shouldn't have done, but it did — and another truth about myself was revealed to me. The Friar nodded and brought me back to the conversation.

"We have much to do. All three of us must hold Hemal; I will contact her and aid her in drawing the strength she needs to rejoin us."

I took one of Hemal's hands and Hammond the other while the Friar gently held her face. I closed my eyes and focused my will. After entering Hammond's mind through my memories I'd forgotten my mental impediment. The block on my body frustrated me; I remained imprisoned within myself.

"It's all right; she will do what is needed."

The Friar might have been right, but that didn't mean I liked the fact. I tried not to show it, though; pride still counted for something. Besides, my time with these two had taught me to accept what I couldn't control with some grace.

On the outside at least.

Hemal's skin felt cool to the touch. With my now stunted senses I barely detected any thread of life within her. Her human shape looked frail and beneath it I saw the impossible geometries of her true form. They still shifted and twisted in a way which hurt to look at. The movement appeared slower than when I'd first arrived in the Garden.

I feared that her skin would burst at any moment. How much longer would she survive in this state? I'd clearly pulled Hammond back none too soon; I wondered how long I had been inside his head.

Hammond's sturdy hand gripped my shoulder, then the Friar's so we formed a complete circle with Hemal at our centre. A moment of stillness passed and then I sensed a push. It was a physical sensation, but something didn't feel right.

The push became a pull; warmth bloomed from Hemal's skin through our hands. My spirit, the sense of me within the shape of my body stretched towards Hemal. The barrier of my body presented no obstacle to this summons.

I tried to focus on the sensation to see if I could emulate the trick. My focus failed and once again frustration surged within me. My anger didn't last; it drained into the surge flowing into Hemal.

At first I enjoyed the sensation, which contained gentle warmth that managed to be both pleasant and calming. I guessed this to be some form of spiritual anaesthetic which masked the shock to the system of our life force being drained. With an effort I opened my eyes and glanced at my companions. Both Hammond and Friar Francis wore blissful expressions on their faces; they reminded me of my experimental phase. They looked stoned, not from the regular stuff, from something special. The finest smoke would expand your awareness; turn you into a drooling savant incapable of speech but capable of witnessing wonders within your own mind.

Ah, fond memories of good times.

Those times had been before I discovered the abyss at the centre of my mind. It existed in all minds, but my connection had always been stronger than anyone else's. I'd always assumed my abilities had caused this. Maybe it stemmed from something more fundamental.

I reached for the answer which floated just out of reach, and then the warmth turned to fire. I'd known fire like this before.

When I'd stolen the miracle it had blazed in every part of my flesh — my punishment for my sin.

It lasted only for a moment and then faded. At the time I felt too relieved to wonder what it meant. The pull on my spirit stopped too and then it struck me how drained I felt. No longer did I experience the tranquillity of the process; now I simply felt weak. My eyelids were too heavy to open.

A brief rest was all I needed.

That shouldn't be too much to ask.

Apparently it was.

A terrible shriek startled me from my slumber. My eyes opened and the others looked about in surprise. Hemal too awoke, although she still looked frail. The echo of the noise reverberated down the tunnel.

The sound had already faded into silence; we all stared into the darkness which stretched beyond sight. With the other way blocked by the earlier collapse it could only have come from one direction.

"What the hell was that?" I asked.

No-one answered me.

I've always had trouble admitting fear, even in the privacy of my own thoughts, but the memory of the scream shivered down my spine with its chill.

In the silence that followed we all stared down the tunnel. What could have made such a sound? Even compared to the screams of a billion dying people it touched something raw inside me. It contained such hunger, such ferocity that even I was impressed by its power.

I looked Hemal in the eye and repeated my question.

"What the hell was that?"

Her voice sounded weak, but I appreciated the improvement on not being able to speak at all.

"I've been told tales of humans, deranged by the transformation of death. They're supposed to live in these tunnels and have done for centuries."

"That scream came from a human?" I didn't believe it — it had sounded like nothing I imagined as being human, more like a dinosaur perhaps. No human could have made such a horrific sound.

Hemal nodded in reply.

"That's the story; I've never seen them for myself..."

"Them?"

I really didn't like the idea of there being more than one thing which made a sound like that.

"I have no idea how many. Until now I didn't even know they really existed. Angels don't use the tunnels. We can transport ourselves throughout creation at will, so we have no need of them."

"Sounds handy, but how many of these things are there?"

"Don't get too excited. I'm afraid souls cannot travel in the same way and I don't know how many of these things there are. Until a few seconds ago they were just a story."

"So what do we do?"

"There's only one way to go," Hammond joined in.

We all looked into the darkness again; the tunnel seemed to smile at us, inviting us into its maw. A fresh shriek, louder this time cut through the shadow.

Chapter 11
In the Darkness

We lacked any practical alternative. There was only direction in which to head. None of us were in great shape and I doubted we would last long in a fight. The alternative of waiting for the shrieking thing to come and get us didn't sit well either.

Hemal told us the little she'd heard about these things. Once they had been human — but warped from the transition. Despite being human even angels considered them like bogeymen, the nearest thing to true evil in creation.

They hunted in the tunnels the other souls had created with their own forms to hide from the angelic raiding parties of both the loyalists and the rebels. Their refuge became a haunt of terror as the dark souls of their own kind hunted them in the pallid light.

The shriekers feasted upon their own kind, growing stronger with each kill. Some claimed the oldest possessed the strength to battle the lesser angels on their own terms. I hoped that wasn't the case with the one whose screech shadowed us through the tunnel.

The creatures delighted in their kills. I assumed there was some truth at the heart of the dark tales of torture and ritualised feeding. I'd always enjoyed horror stories, but I didn't fancy being the victim in one.

Despite the tales we moved further into the darkness. Where else could we go? The pale light from the walls provided enough light for us to navigate, but the echoes of the shrieks made it difficult to determine how far away the creature was from us. At least there only seemed to be one of them.

Even our slow movement drained us. We didn't hear the terrible shriek again, so after an hour of cautious movement we stopped to rest.

The tunnel had run straight. I sensed that it angled downward a little, but not by much. The soft glow from the walls provided enough light to make each other out across the width of the tunnel.

"How can we find this last true demon?" I asked Hemal. She appeared stronger, but still far from her normal self.

"We need to make contact with some friends."

"Who?"

"Other angels who might have more information."

"Might? That doesn't sound very certain."

She shrugged.

"The demons are a mystery which we've never really understood — so much so they were feared by all of us."

"I know, and that's why you killed them all, but how can you be sure one still exists?"

"I can't, but there have been enough rumours through the ages, not just here in heaven, but appearances amongst your kind as well."

"What do you mean?"

"There are people in your history who wielded extraordinary gifts, beyond even those of your line."

"I thought they were possessed by angels?"

"We assumed the same for centuries until a few of us investigated and we didn't find any angels responsible."

"So you believe they were one of the demons?"

"Not at first, but some of the actions warranted deeper investigation. Certain humans performed miracles, changes to the world which couldn't be committed by talented humans or even possessed ones."

"Why not? I thought the potential existed inside us all?"

"The physical universe is built from rules; all life forms within the universe must obey those rules. You can stretch them, even bend them to your will, but you cannot break them and neither can we."

The Friar interrupted with his own question.

"More importantly, how can this demon help us?"

"He can't, but I hope he can help us find a way to communicate with God who can restore your world and your people."

The Friar looked doubtful, but let it lie. I had more immediate concerns.

"Before we can find this true demon we need to get out of this tunnel. We've not seen any sign of an exit since we entered. Where will it take us?"

"I don't know."

I'd hoped for something a bit more useful.

"All right, how do we get out of here?"

"We follow the tunnel and see where it leads us."

Hammond stood, using the wall to support himself as he rose. We followed his lead and headed once again into the gloom. Our footsteps and breathing (I still didn't understand why we felt the need) were the only sounds we heard.

We kept walking for what seemed like hours, and we stopped only when the tunnel ended.

Chapter 12
Domain

The tunnel simply ended. It was sealed by the same material that formed the walls.

"Why would the tunnel end here?"

It seemed a reasonable question; unfortunately nobody had a satisfactory answer. And to be honest it freaked me out. Why would a tunnel just end like that?

I placed my hand against the blockage, which felt warm to the touch the same as the other walls. Like resin it held a rich lustre even in the poor light.

"These tunnels were made by humans?" the Friar asked.

"They're constructed from humans, or more accurately human souls, they transform themselves into part of creation," Hemal replied.

"Maybe the next one changed his mind and returned to his normal form?"

"It's possible."

She sounded doubtful though and that didn't enhance my calm at all

Hammond then entered with a more worrying question.

"What about the shrieking thing? We haven't passed any other tunnels, so it's somewhere in here with us."

A concern to be sure. I didn't want to meet anything capable of such a horrible sound any time soon, especially with my abilities confined within my head.

Friar Francis considered Hammond's question. "If they can change form, then maybe they can alter the layout of the tunnels as well?"

"It's possible."

Well that was just great. Here we were trapped in the tunnel with a demented howling soul-eating creature which could apparently reconfigure the tunnels around us.

"There must be a way out."

I was pleased to see Hammond's usual positive attitude return. Of course, his training and a lifetime of action and service had prepared him for adversity like this. I also remembered that he enjoyed it; in fact he thrived on it.

I watched him test the wall, searching for any sign of weakness. I'd already tried the same without success. Without tools of any description it proved a fruitless endeavour. I watched him anyway.

The Friar watched him as well, but his mind appeared elsewhere and eventually he spoke.

"If they created a tunnel can we not do the same?"

As Hammond probed the wall, Hemal closed her eyes. She still looked weak; our strength helped, but hadn't restored her fully. After all a thimble of petrol doesn't fill a truck's fuel tank. She opened her eyes and frowned.

"That might work — I would try but I don't think it is possible for angels. I know we can't create here in the way that we can in Heaven."

"I can try," the Friar said. "Tell me what to do."

"Wait a minute," I interrupted. "Where will the tunnel take us to?"

"To the surface is probably best," Hemal replied.

"Is that really a good idea? We have no idea what the situation is up there and not to forget that the world fell down up there."

"I can guide him through the process and see through him what is happening before he opens a tunnel."

"How can you be sure he'll be able to reach the surface? How far away is it?"

"It doesn't matter; distance isn't the issue, only the will and the determination to reach your target."

In our current state that wasn't what I wanted to hear. The Friar possessed deep reserves so if it had to be anyone ... screw that — it should have been me. I didn't enjoy the feeling of being useless. That feeling was usually reserved for my victims not me. Only I had been neutered and that still pained me.

"So why hasn't whoever formed this tunnel reached somewhere?"

"They probably lacked the will or the strength, or maybe the person they connected to changed or left."

"Can't you create a tunnel? You told me that angels built Heaven."

"Heaven and Hell yes, Eden no. God crafted Eden specifically for human souls."

"So we can change Eden?"

"Yes, it's a realm for human souls. A few of us believe that angels should never have entered."

I didn't like the sound of that; something felt wrong here. I cursed my inability to leave my mind and probe our surroundings. I didn't think Hemal would lead us astray, but there seemed to be something she had missed.

"We have no other option. Hammond, lend Friar Francis your strength in case he needs it."

Hammond nodded and placed his hands on the Friar's shoulders.

"How can I help?" I asked her.

"Keep alert; we'll all have to concentrate to build the tunnel."

In other words I couldn't provide any useful help and again that hurt, not because I liked helping people, but I have always been useful.

I shrugged in response. No point in sharing my concern at my new-found weakness. The appearance of power is sometimes as good as the real thing.

"Place your hands on the wall and focus your mind," Hemal told the Friar. "You should be able to detect the soul forming the tunnel."

"She senses me."

"Don't communicate with her; maintaining the integrity of the tunnel requires the creator's focus. Disrupting that focus might collapse this tunnel."

"All right. I'm passing through carefully. She's not resisting. I wonder why she built a tunnel to nowhere."

"That's good, but don't start being curious — she can't be distracted, remember?"

"Understood."

"Be careful; don't push too hard. Allow yourself to drift through."

"I'm at the edge. I can't see anything."

"Hold there — don't push forward yet. The void you see isn't what it seems. In your universe you delve inwards to see the smallest of things. It is the space between these tiny things that defines your reality."

I remembered the Friar teaching me that nothing is perfect; there is a flaw to everything. Using those flaws creates levers which can be forced to make things happen.

"Here things are very different — the opposite in fact. What you see isn't the space between things; it is more, so much more."

"I don't understand."

I agreed with the Friar, I didn't understand Hemal's words either.

Hemal considered for a moment before continuing. "Your universe is constructed from a finite number of dimensions. Within those dimensions physical objects interact, attracting and repelling to construct a larger whole. It is those gaps which define your universe.

"Human philosophers had long discussed the duality of nature, of energy and matter, of good and evil, light and dark. In truth it boils down to those two actions, attraction and repulsion."

It made some sense to me, but didn't explain the different nature of Heaven.

"The universe you know is limited, but here creation is everything. Think back to the instant of your death and your transition from the chaotic life of flesh into the immortal soul you've become."

"Ok," the Friar replied.

"In the transition you passed from the life you lived, through everything that you could have been and ended up as the being you now are. Here creation is the same. It is everything that it could be; it just happens to be in a state that it currently rests in."

"How does that help me grasp the reality of what is here to form the tunnel?"

"To comprehend this reality you do not try to understand how it is constructed. You must not try to reduce it to its component parts. It is more than it is. Rather than tighten your focus allow it to expand."

"All right, I'm expanding my awareness. It feels strange, I can see the wall — I can even touch the wall. I hear you speaking, but my inner sense detects nothing."

"It does, you just don't realise. When you look into the night sky you see the stars. Focus on a small point and all you see is the darkness of space. Expand your view and you see the jewels of the sky; expand even further and you see the majesty of the galaxy. Widen your view further still and you'll see the whole universe."

"Ok."

The Friar concentrated. I stared at his back while Hammond held onto his shoulder and Hemal stood next to them. Although I looked at them, I didn't really see them. I thought about Hemal's instructions to the Friar. I wondered whether it applied in some way to my own predicament and, if so, how?

"Oh my God!"

The Friar's voice sounded full of wonder.

"I can see it all."

"Don't reach too far, Friar, or you will be lost."

"I can see the sun; it shines down upon a river. I know this river."

"Wait, that's not right." Hemal's voice carried the concern visible on her face. "Pull him back, Hammond — something is not right here."

The smell of hot desert air surrounded us, and the tunnel opened like the mouth of a giant serpent. Bright yellow light warm from the sun's rays consumed us, and in an instant it swallowed us whole.

Chapter 13
The Sun King

It took time for our eyes to adjust to the intense brightness of the sunlight and reveal an unexpected scene.

I recognised it immediately; who wouldn't? It is after all one of the most distinctive skylines in all of history, although what I beheld didn't look like a rundown tourist attraction. Instead I saw ancient Egypt at the height of its power. I'd never visited the last standing wonder of the world in person, but I'd seen it often enough on TV and in films.

The vision before me reminded me of the magnificent epics on the big screen. It looked larger than life, greater than it would have done in real life.

"How is this possible?" I asked.

Even Hemal looked awestruck.

"No angel has ever seen one of these domains. It's beautiful."

I had to agree with her: it was beautiful. The river Nile snaked through a pristine desert, wide lush banks of verdant green spread like a garden into the dunes. On the river magnificent barges sailed with the current, and although they were far in the distance I made out small figures dancing in celebration on the polished decks.

Along the river stood tall statues of exotically-headed Gods, who watched the river with stern animal faces. At regular intervals along the banks carved paths the colour of bleached bone formed avenues leading to small temples.

Each temple was surrounded by colonnades and trees, the green of their leaves vibrant against the sand-coloured stone. Birds with bright plumage flocked around the temple, their songs travelling across the desert.

"So are these domains formed in the same way as the tunnels?" I asked the angel.

"No, well yes, sort of."

"A nice clear cut answer. It's difficult to explain."

"Try me and make it quick. We have no idea what's waiting for us here." "We first suspected something when large populations of souls disappeared from Eden. It seemed more likely when we realised that the vanished shared the same culture or beliefs. We didn't understand why at first, but we uncovered rumours from souls who joined our forces."

"So they created their own afterlife?"

"Exactly and not just the ancient Egyptians. If enough people believe in something and they are able to work together then they can create whatever they want."

"That's pretty cool."

I remembered my own creation, the Parisian cafe by the abyss, and wondered if I'd be able do the same here. A movement near the river below interrupted my thoughts.

"It looks like we have company," I said to my companions and pointed towards a group of robed people walking towards us. The path they walked upon extended of its own volition across the sand in our direction.

"Let's hope the locals are friendly," Hammond said.

The sight of the approaching party pushed that uncomfortable thought aside. I counted a dozen people. All but one of them appeared to be soldiers, and they wore short pristine white tunics which exposed well-toned muscles on their arms and legs. Burnished bronze armour protected their shins, forearms and chests although the ornate markings indicated it was more ceremonial than for protection.

They all marched at a measured pace. At the head walked one whom I assumed to be a priest. They approached deliberately and followed the path as it unfurled before them.

The priest wore long flowing white robes, and upon his head I saw a strange crown, more like a flower than a headdress.

"I hope you're right," I said to Hammond, but as their faces came into view I recognised only grim determination. I turned to

Hemal, hoping she would know what to do. A slight shrug of her shoulders ended that hope.

"Friar?"

He shrugged too. "I've studied some of their history, but I don't know a great deal."

"What about the basics? How to say 'hello', or 'we come in peace'?"

"I'm afraid not. Their history provided an interesting diversion, but not essential to my life's devotion."

"Well, we have a High Priest and his guards striding towards us and he has a pissed off look on his face. It would be good to be able to say something."

"He's not a high priest."

Hammond's words surprised me.

"What?"

"He's not a High Priest; he's more like a magician."

"I don't see the distinction."

"For the Egyptians religion was a practical thing, their afterlife simply a continuation of their lives. Their magicians prepared them for their passing."

"How do you know this?"

"You get a surprising amount of time with little to do but read while on deployment."

"All right, now do you remember anything useful, like what do we say to this guy?"

The big man raised his hands, "Sorry, I read about them, I didn't learn their language or customs."

"Wonderful. I guess we play it by ear."

The leader came to a halt. His men fanned out behind him in a loose arc, their hands resting on the short curved swords on their hips.

"It has been many years since anyone passed into our realm."

I was so surprised I understood his words that I didn't respond at first. This didn't seem to bother the man, and he waited patiently for me to speak.

"You speak English?"

"I don't understand what you mean," he replied.

"You understand what I am saying."

"Of course."

"And I understand what you are saying."

"Naturally." His determined look faded a little; maybe he thought he was dealing with an idiot. It returned when he looked at Hemal. "That thing is not welcome here."

"Wait, what? Hemal, she's fine."

"It leaves or it will be banished."

I glanced at Hemal, who shrugged again. "I don't know how to. I don't even know how we got in here."

"You were invited," the Magician said. "That was not." He gestured towards Hemal and with a dull pop a dark light surrounded her. That sounds impossible, I know — darkness after all is an absence of light, but what I saw was an emission of blackness, a negative glow which wrapped around the angel.

She screamed.

I stepped forward, "Wait, we will all go. Please — we do not know how we came to be here. If you send her then you must send us too."

"That is incorrect; it will be sent away," and with that command the darkness collapsed, taking Hemal from sight. Her scream faded. "You will remain here. It has been many, many years since a heart was last weighed and now we have three.

"It is a joyous day."

Chapter 14
Heavy Hearts

As Hemal vanished from sight I launched myself at the magician. Hammond followed a heartbeat behind me, and the Friar less than a second after him. The Magician calmly stepped back. I should have reached him yet somehow I failed.

The guards stepped in. They didn't rush and it shouldn't have been possible for them to intercept me but almost without moving they grabbed me. I struggled against their grip. Although still weak from restoring Hemal it proved a futile effort, but it didn't stop me from trying. I tried to unleash my will at the three soldiers who held me; in extremis I hoped that this time I would pass through the barrier of my body.

I didn't.

So I fought the old-fashioned way, not that it really made any difference. They smothered my efforts with insulting ease. The same happened for the Friar and Hammond. Hammond's training and bulk made him harder to subdue, but four of the bronze-skinned soldiers managed it without sustaining any injury.

The magician stepped back into view, his face calm. He showed no anger at our resistance, and I guessed that maybe it wasn't uncommon. Even for believers having one's heart weighed probably didn't rate as a pleasant prospect.

"Most of those who arrive here struggle against the inevitability of their judgement," he told us, confirming my suspicion, "but it is not us you should fight against — we are only the caretakers of this place."

"So you say, but you are the ones restraining us."

"Everyone who enters this land of the dead must be judged. There can be no exceptions; all of us here have had our hearts measured before the Sun King."

He motioned towards the path. What choice did we have but to step onto its surface and follow it down to the river?

They allowed us to set the pace, which created the illusion that it was a pleasant stroll under the summer sun. As we approached the river we heard sounds of life, gentle voices singing in praise of their god, the Sun King. The river lapped against the reeds lining its banks. Up close we saw the barges made from rich wood, inlaid with gold glittering in the sun.

The sails billowed in the breeze that kept us cool despite the sun's efforts. This could have been a perfect summer stroll bar the fact we walked towards our doom.

More accurately, my doom.

I didn't know whether this weighing of our hearts was a rigged game or not. In a fit of optimism I assumed that it wasn't — in which case Hammond should be ok. He had lived a good life after all.

Then it occurred to me that I didn't have any idea by what criteria our hearts would be judged. I questioned the Magician about what would happen. He seemed happy to talk, but didn't provide any of the details I wanted.

"All will be explained during the ritual. As yours are the first hearts to be weighed in centuries the Sun King himself will officiate at the ceremony and he will tell you in person."

That didn't fill me with the honour I assumed he thought it should.

I wanted to know more, but I'd have to wait. We continued along the river and the illusion of a golden paradise persisted. Birds flew through the air, their song light upon the breeze.

We passed the first avenue. I looked along the tree-lined path towards the temple there. Closer to the buildings the hieroglyphs upon the columns and walls became visible, if not comprehensible. With vibrant colours they described knowledge and worship. For a second I focused and almost grasped the secrets they held, but then we walked on and the vision disappeared.

For over an hour we walked along the bank, following the path until a new temple, greater than any of the others, came into view. Here stood our destination. Its size made it appear closer than it was, and another two hours passed until we reached its grand entrance.

The three of us talked along the way and our escorts didn't mind. Our first concern was for Hemal. We hoped she had only been banished and not to a fate more fatal. I asked the Magician, who tried to set our minds at ease — but he wouldn't explain why the angel wasn't welcome in this domain.

We talked about the upcoming ceremony. Hammond told us the little he remembered from his reading. The ancient Egyptians believed that when a man died his heart was weighed by the gods and if it balanced then his afterlife would be paradise.

Hearts that weighed heavy with evil would be condemned to the underworld. Most people didn't share my flexible view of the world, so I doubted that I would be judged according to my own standards.

Our conversation petered out as the grand pyramid filled our view and we all felt more than a little awed by the sight. The pyramid gleamed in the sun like a beacon to Heaven.

I appreciated the irony of that thought.

We slowed as we approached. Our guards now set the pace and we moved in time to a ceremonial procession. Without a word being said the ritual had begun.

Through the shadow of the pyramid we marched; out of the sun the air chilled. More soldiers and giant trees lined the broad avenue. There were hundreds of soldiers, all dressed in the uniform of white and gold. Unlike our escorts they all carried spears taller than the guards who wielded them.

When we reached the entrance they all slammed the base of their spears against the ground in unison. The sound rippled around the expanse like a roll of thunder. As the sound decayed we entered the pyramid.

The interior gleamed with white marble which reflected the light from a thousand oil lamps. The cool air contrasted with the glare we'd come from. Our footsteps echoed in the cavernous space. The air smelled of burnt spices which tasted warm as I breathed.

Between the painted columns lay pools of still water, and around these groups of men and women watched silently, dressed in variations of the white tunics. More soldiers lined the path leading to the carved stone steps.

No-one made a sound as we walked towards the steps. A boy sat in a golden throne at the top. The Magician instructed us to stop at the foot of the steps with a simple gesture. He then bowed and addressed the boy king.

"My Lord, I bring the newly departed."

The Sun King (he was only a boy!) nodded, the motion small, but that of one used to being in command. He then stood and gazed down upon us, and as he stood everyone except us bowed to their knees.

"It has been too long since anyone has entered our great realm. It is with celebration we welcome these three. I will weigh their hearts and as has been done for millennia their destinies will be decided.

"Like the rest of us here in this place who have received their judgement, we hope they will find their hearts are light and their lives can be spent here in praise of the Gods."

He might have looked young, but his voice rang deep with age. How long had this boy been king? I wasn't keen on the suggestion that the good result would be trapped here praising their Gods for eternity.

"Wait — we're not of your people."

A blow from one of the soldiers stopped my words and forced me to my knees. The king didn't seem perturbed by my outburst.

"We have people from many races here, including those from the northlands such as you. All are judged and only the deserving remain. The rest are cast into the underworld where they will fade from existence."

I didn't like the sound of that either. Perhaps the good result wouldn't be so bad after all.

A new sound came from one side. Four porters carried the most ornate scales I had ever seen. This would be the tool of our judgement. They placed the balance on the marble near us and withdrew into the shadows.

"Bring the first one."

At their king's command two of the guards led Hammond to the oversized scales and forced him to kneel before it.

Chapter 15
Dark Secret

The guards placed Hammond's hands beside the scales. My sight blanked for a second and then I saw Hammond's life. Like some form of augmented reality I witnessed Hammond's life and yet still saw him kneeling by the scales. I'd already searched through his memories, so I saw nothing to surprise me.

What I did find interesting was the interplay with the scales. When the darker memories played the balance shifted, dropping on the right. When I first noticed the movement I also discovered something else: a beating heart appeared on the pan. I checked Hammond, but his chest appeared intact, and his face wore the strain of the experience. Whatever power dredged through his memories did so more intrusively than mine.

For the happier, purer memories the pan lifted, the balance shifting in what I assumed was the positive direction. I glanced around and everyone was rapt, focused on Hammond's life. I don't know how long it took. Although the memories ran in chronological order, it wasn't a second-by-second recounting of his life; it passed through all of his major decisions.

At first I thought that it used the same mechanism as the transformation of the soul. However I soon realised it differed in that it cared only about what Hammond had actually done in his life. It weighed his choices — not the repercussions of the choices he failed to make.

The show ended with his death at the hands of the Antichrist. The events after his death were not replayed; only the choices in his life mattered. With his death he slumped to the ground and his hands slipped from the scales. The King looked down onto the scales and when he saw the heart pan settled higher than its counterpart, he smiled.

"This man's heart has been judged as worthy. By treading an honest path he has earned his place here in service with the Gods who have guided him."

The two guards bowed to their king and gently carried Hammond away. His face looked pale and drawn, and the experience had clearly drained him. They laid him upon a low seat away from the steps.

"Now for the second. Bring the tall one."

The Friar's guards took his arms and moved towards the scales. To my surprise the Friar resisted. I saw fear on his face. I had never seen him afraid. Concerned on occasion — perhaps even apprehensive — but here I witnessed real fear. I couldn't imagine why. Surely he had little to fear from the weighing.

His desperation allowed him to slip from the guards, but only for a moment. With slow and deliberate movements (but did I sense something slip beneath the moments as they passed?) two more guards intervened and dragged him to the scales.

He continued to resist until the moment his hands touched the scales and then he froze. From the trembling muscles I guessed that he continued attempting to resist, but the revelations were inevitable.

In a day full of surprises the heart appearing on the pan and then immediately sinking so low it clattered against its mounting proved to be the greatest. What the Hell!

The Friar's early memories lay heavy with darkness. I'd never looked into his mind beyond the exercises back in his special prison where he trained me in the use of my abilities. I'd always imagined him to be a learned man, to have come up through academia. In part I was right, but also so far from the truth it stunned me.

His early life was one of privilege: private school, expensive home and anything he wanted, but it came with a price. From an early age, soon after he first started school, he took part in rituals.

We witnessed those dark rituals of pain and blood. His father worshipped evil and strange gods, ones willing to provide power and influence in return for worship. With the revelations I'd learned I didn't think such things were possible, but it seemed there was indeed some truth to these practices.

The Friar's memories didn't confirm if such entities were real — it showed only the acts committed by those who believed they were. I'd never shied away from brutality in my life but the scenes I saw in his memories were something special to behold.

At first he only watched the torture and murder; step by step his father inducted him deeper into the mysteries. Unlike his father the boy possessed true talent. He heard the voices as they really were and not the delusions which invited his father to fulfil his perverted desires.

The powers spoke to the boy and promised him a future greater than that which his father offered, although a sacrifice would be needed. Years passed. The boy feared his father, but the power kept whispering promises.

Eventually the boy's will weakened and he agreed to do the deed. Fratricide is the greatest crime to the ancient Egyptians and a horrified gasp swept through the throne room as the teenage boy murdered his father on the blood-soaked altar.

More atrocities followed and as the boy reached puberty the power aided his development — but unknown to him the power had its own plan. It required a strong mind and prepared to seize the Friar as its own vessel. One final sacrifice would complete the transfer, and it would be the most dread murder of all.

Salvation came in the same form that saved me when I'd been captured by Lazarus. A team of black clad holy ninjas stormed the estate and shot the boy before he killed the squalling babe. Two priests accompanied the assault team, one Jesuit and the other from the Dominican Order.

The Friar's road back to the light proved a long and difficult one. He'd experienced the supernatural so believing in God came easy, but he found it more difficult to come to terms with the horrific crimes he'd committed. It took years, but the two priests remained patient and didn't give up on him.

Everyone in the room experienced the Friar's feelings as he discovered normal human emotions. Guilt hit him first and the hardest. He attempted suicide on many occasions and had to be restrained for days at a time to prevent him hurting himself.

The priests worked with him for several years. He gradually spent more time with other people. Under their guidance he reached a point where he realised that he could assuage his guilt by trying to redeem himself. He didn't believe that would be possible, but to live a life trying would be worth more than doing nothing at all.

The decision became the pivotal moment of his life and on the scales the right hand pan lifted — not by much, but enough to spark a gasp around the assembled watchers.

He decided to join the Dominican Order: another key decision which ultimately caused our paths to intersect. Step by dogged step he joined the battle against the church's enemies. It didn't mean he always fought against evil, but he did so often enough that the heart lifted by the tiniest amount.

A litany of battles and interventions raised his heart higher and by the time his memories reached his first encounter with me it had levelled. Convincing me to battle Lazarus pushed it even higher and seeing that made me proud.

That was an unusual emotion for me. I often experienced pride in what I did, not so often in what people did with me.

With the Friar's life story complete he ended in the light side of the balance. The King and his courtiers stood stunned. It was tight, but the balance was on his side and everyone was amazed. Including me.

A few seconds passed before the King spoke. The age in his voice vanished in his excitement.

"This man's heart has been weighed and found to be just. His path through to death was a long and tortuous one, but by the end he lived in the grace of the light. He has earned his place here with the Gods."

The Friar had collapsed and I heard him weeping. His guards carefully moved him and laid him near Hammond who took his old friend in his arms to comfort him.

The King nodded at the sight, then turned to look at me and instructed me to face the scales for judgement.

Chapter 16
Judgement Day

Of course it occurred to me to resist, but on this rare occasion I understood it would pointless and I had my pride. The Egyptians owned this domain; I still didn't understand how they moved so quickly without any apparent effort. It offered me a puzzle I would have liked to have spent more time with, but I had my judgement to face.

Deep down I knew that the other reason I didn't resist was curiosity. I wondered what would happen — well, I knew what would happen, but what would the experience be like? What can I say? I'm a sucker for a new experience.

I knelt before the golden scales and placed my hands on them and cold shock swept through me. The scales twitched as my heart appeared on the right hand pan. It didn't sink straight away — I wasn't born evil, I took a few years to grow into it.

And what a journey it became.

It still seemed strange placing myself in those terms. My transformation had opened my eyes and the weighing of my heart did the same, but in a more brutal fashion. Although they had a similar effect they held opposite sides of the spectrum.

Death laid bare the truth of my life and exposed not only what I was, but the mystery of what I could have been. This wasn't a rerun of my life. Here every decision was scrutinised and weighed for the contribution I'd made to the world.

The early years passed with barely a tremor in the scales. The death of the fox, dashing its brains out by the rock in my hand caused the first drop. Not by a lot — the world didn't care all that much about a dead animal — although that was just the start. Further smaller dips followed in rapid succession as I discovered my powers and experimented with manipulation.

The next significant dip took place with the seduction (subjugation) of Miss Clarke, a fond memory indeed and I wished to linger with these memories a while but my actions slipped like a passing heartbeat into the past as soon as they were judged.

I watched as the pan sank lower towards its mount while the years rolled by for all those assembled to see. I saw the rare lift in the balance, but for the most part it dropped downwards.

No real surprise there.

Visions of my choices paraded past. The experiments in inner exploration and self-medication triggered fond memories and, compared to some of my earlier activities, weighed the scales little. That surprised me, although with more objective eyes I realised that while some mishaps may have occurred, for that time I had lost my desire for tormenting people.

We shared dark experiences, but everyone had been a willing participant until we fell too deep into the abyss. A single death sparked a change in my fortunes greater than even that of my mother's death.

On grey streets I wandered, obscured in the filth of homelessness. A strange choice — I could have grabbed more at will, but I wallowed in the misery of it. Looking back I realised that I experienced a perverse pride in my self-imposed exile.

Up until then I'd flirted with evil, played with my abilities for personal reasons and selfish gain. It could be said that at the heart of all evil is the worm of selfish desire. In my spiralling bitterness I discovered a new pleasure — more than that, it became my devotion. It started as judgement. I burrowed into people's thoughts as they passed me by, then took what I found in their heads and turned it against them

It didn't end there, of course. What started as an exercise in poetic justice degenerated into sport — a game which I eventually tired of, but not until I'd ruined thousands of lives. I then thought of a glorious and violent plan for suicide. I'd grown tired of life and was eager to embrace oblivion, but not alone.

I'd first met Hammond in the prison where I intended to enact my plan; he'd been a guard there. I'd also met the Friar at that time and they had showed me a world I'd never imagined.

They recruited me to take out Lazarus and from that point on things just got ever weirder. It wasn't easy but I killed him and stole the miracle. I'd saved the world with that act, but also gained immortality.

The scales lifted for a brief moment with Lazarus' demise, then sank lower again when the fire from the miracle coursed through my body.

The remainder of my life flashed by quickly. The decision to kill the Antichrist again lifted the scales, but only by a fraction. Perhaps it would have been more if I'd succeeded in my task.

Memories of my death and the agony of the miracle being torn from my body punctuated the end of the judgement and my heart sat heavy in the pan of the scales. A gaunt quiet filled the throne room. The Sun King in his deceptively young body stared at me.

I saw all I needed to see in his eyes, but as he prepared to speak, Hammond's voice interrupted him.

"Wait, we need him! He can help us restore the world."

The boy king shook his head.

"The world is just fine; here we are protected by our gods. We cannot and will not anger them by ignoring their word. Judgement has been made, and for a soul as dark as this even the underworld isn't a fit enough punishment."

"That may be true, but he can save everything."

"He has already failed and we do not need saving. You should rejoice for you have found your way to paradise."

"What if we offered our own places in exchange?"

The boy king reflected for a moment. He glanced at the magician who responded with a discreet shake of his head.

"Judgement cannot be traded. Your places here have been earned through lives well lived, as has his place in the eternal dark."

"There must be a way."

"It speaks well of you to hope for such."

Now the Friar entered the exchange with a question of his own.

"Can only a single heart be weighed at once?"

I immediately understood where he was going with this and I understood it would be a bad idea. I tried to speak, to stop the Friar before he made his offer, but the judgement had drained me of my strength and reduced my voice to less than a whisper.

The king glanced again at his advisors. One of them shrugged. The option appeared open, but would the king go for it?

"There's no rule saying it has to be one, but tradition dictates that it is a man's life that is judged. Why should his be different?"

"We need him to fix what is broken. Do you comprehend what has happened?"

"The destruction of the Earth. We may be isolated here, but we are not out of touch. However it is not our world; our world is here and safe from the forces outside."

"Once the humans in Eden are destroyed the angels will come here."

"They can try. We are protected."

"With this man's help we can undo what has been done."

"Why should we care?"

That puzzled the Friar, although I understood what the king meant.

"What do you mean?"

"This is our domain; we exist with our gods and follow our ways as we have for thousands of years. You are the first to enter for many centuries. We are secure here."

"Maybe, but what if you aren't?"

"Explain."

"The world was separate in its own universe. Now it has been ripped apart and dropped on Eden. Michael and Lucifer intend to destroy all of humanity, including those already passed."

"Our gods and our magic will protect us; none may enter our realm without our leave."

"What if the rules have changed?"

That gave the boy king pause for thought.

"I cannot just let this man go. The laws must be obeyed."

The Friar nodded.

"Laws should be adhered to; all we ask is that our hearts be used to offset his."

This was a bad idea — I still lacked the ability to object out loud — but the Friar still had faith even if Hammond didn't. Faith in what though I didn't know.

"And if your hearts are not enough, you will be cast into the underworld with him."

"We understand."

His voice was firm, and matched by Hammond's affirmative nod.

"Then it is agreed. Take your places next to your friend."

The Friar and Hammond knelt down beside me and placed their hands upon the scales. Their hearts appeared upon the pan next to mine and it lifted. For a moment I thought it would be enough. I should have known better. My earlier doubts had proved correct; the scales didn't balance.

I couldn't tell whether the king was pleased by the result or not, either way he still condemned the three of us to the underworld.

Chapter 17
Lost in Shadow

One moment we knelt within the throne room of the Sun King, the next we drowned in darkness. This wasn't the black of night; more than just the mere absence of light, it was absolute black. I sensed the Friar and Hammond beside me and turned to look.

I saw them in the dark only as vague forms, ghosts of shadow. It was the oddest thing I had ever seen. There was no light, not even a monochrome brightening. It looked more like a sonar return; I sensed the edges of them.

"What the hell was that?" I demanded.

"We couldn't leave you on your own," the Friar replied.

"Why?"

"We can't help you if we're still up there."

"Help? I don't see how we can achieve anything here."

I looked around again; everything remained pure black. A chill encased my body, draining it of warmth.

"Where are we?"

"In the underworld, I assume."

"Very clever. Hammond, do you remember anything about this place?"

"Not much. I read that it's place of darkness and loss. Souls are condemned to wander here until they are completely drained and fade from existence."

"Wonderful."

Already I felt a little bit colder, or was it my imagination? I asked myself if this would be how it ended: lost in the dark with the cold slowly draining my strength until the end. I'd imagined something more dramatic, but at least at the end I'd attain the oblivion I'd sought for so long.

I wondered how time worked here, if it did at all. In the end I decided it didn't really matter.

The touch of Hammond's hand on my shoulder returned me to my senses. The warmth of it scalded my flesh.

"Snap out of it," he chided. "We need to find our way out of here."

"Where? How do we even know where to go?"

"We don't, but we won't find anything by standing around."

He was right of course.

I glanced at the Friar and noticed a pained expression on his face. Hammond followed my look and grimaced in sympathy.

"Be thankful you can't sense the remnants around us," Hammond told me.

"What do you mean?"

"It seems I might have been wrong. Nothing truly dies here. The souls grow weaker, drained by the chill from the fabric of this realm."

I looked around, failing once again to expand my awareness. I don't mind admitting that really pissed me off.

"Trust me; you don't want to hear what he can. The air moves with the wisps of those no longer strong enough to maintain their form."

"So what happens to them?"

"They keep fading, but the real horror is that they will never truly die. Most have diminished so much their anguish is all that remains."

The Friar had always been more sensitive than Hammond. Hammond was an open book — strong in his faith once, but never skilled with mental abilities.

"Can you hear them?"

He shrugged.

"Faintly, but I can tell that the Friar is only just holding it together. His thoughts are leaking into my mind and he can hear them all; most of the souls condemned here have lost their form and only a few remain strong enough to exist with any coherence. They have survived by feeding on the others."

73

I wished that I could hear them; being cut off from my awareness diminished me in a way I hadn't experienced before. On top of that the silence of this dark realm gave me the creeps. This presented something new and to be honest quite horrifying. I didn't mind the darkness; but the utter silence was something quite different. No life existed here and I feared this would be how it ended.

What can you do in a situation like that?

Sure, I experienced some temptation to let the silence and cold take me. Pride, my familiar source of so much anguish and strength kept me going. I would keep going, but the chill smothering us begged to differ.

Focus on something else.

"Where are they?"

"Keeping their distance; they'll wait until we're weaker."

"How do you know this?"

"Some of the souls still have enough strength to speak and the Friar managed to pick them out amongst the cacophony."

"And he believes them? They could be lying."

"True, but there's no way to be sure. I do know that I'm weaker than when we first arrived."

I did too.

"So we're up against the clock," I said after some consideration. "Has he been able to learn anything to help us escape?"

"Maybe; he's seen a vision a mountain that reaches into the sky."

"And that helps us how?"

"Apparently the rest of the realm is flat. It's the only landmark in existence."

I didn't like the sound of this. How could we trust the voices? On the other hand what else did we have to go on? The Friar looked like he might collapse at any moment; we needed to get out of this underworld while we still had the strength.

"How do we find this mountain?"

"We follow the light."

He pointed into the distance and I saw it. I didn't know how I hadn't noticed it before. A white dot in the overwhelming darkness, it didn't look like a light, more like a hole in the black. With no features for reference I had no idea how far away we were.

The dark surrounded us and provided no other clue as to where we should go. I couldn't even see the mountain that Hammond spoke of, just the tiny hole high in the sky. So we walked towards the light and supported the Friar between us.

We walked for hours and in all that time the Friar didn't say a thing, although he moaned every now and then. When he moaned his body twitched and we had to adjust our grip to prevent him from falling.

The silence gnawed at me almost as much as the eternal cold. Only when either of us spoke did anything break the silence. No ambience at all might not sound much like torture, but you would be surprised.

The cold ground sapped our strength with every step and after a while my feet started to hurt. Our minds had created clothes and shoes wrapped around the shapes of our former lives. With the constant chill our attention wavered, and all of our focus was needed just to put one foot in front of the other.

When the pain became too much we stopped and checked the wounds which ruined our feet. Our shoes had disintegrated and our feet worn ragged. Once again the memories of our bodies proved to be a weakness that hampered our progress.

We rested and focused our wills to rebuild the protection for our feet. By the time we stopped again the frozen ground had new wounds.

On one occasion when we stopped we glimpsed a shadow in the darkness. It looked like a man, but it was difficult to be certain. It followed us for a while with a lean and predatory gait. Hammond held the Friar when I tried to approach the lone figure and talk to it, but it quickly retreated into the black as I drew close.

Chapter 18
Reaching for the Sky

A lifetime ago I watched a documentary about a death march. Prisoners marched across the frozen tundra, and when they became too weak to walk they fell into the snow and froze to death. Hammond might have been used to marching from his time with the marines, but I wasn't.

We no longer stopped to rest. Sitting on the ground weakened us more than walking onward — although you couldn't really call it walking anymore. We lurched forward like zombies with the Friar balanced between us.

He too grew weaker; his skin burned to the touch and he trembled in our grip. The few utterances he made became quieter each time. The cold eroded the shield which imprisoned me inside my body. I still couldn't expand my awareness, but it did allow the voices in.

Hungry whispers in the wind frayed my senses and I decided that I preferred the gaunt silence. In fact, I would have given anything to have returned to not hearing the ghosts of the damned.

At first I listened to the voices in an attempt to make sense of them. Most seemed no more than screams — wails of despair and anguish. I caught scraps of voices amongst the flood and some of them spoke of the mountain.

They hadn't lied. We now saw the mountain tall and daunting ahead of us. Its magnificence dwarfed us. It also provided hope which enabled us to keep dragging our torn feet across the frozen ground. Each step remained a blazing agony; even so we continued our march to the mountain.

Every second and with each step the voices screamed and gibbered. I found no respite. I tried withdrawing inside my mind and that silenced the voices for a while until Hammond slapped me awake. He lacked the strength to carry both of us.

Some of the stronger voices begged to be released from their torment. I didn't know how to help them. I couldn't even help myself; it took all of my will just to keep moving forward.

Hammond too now heard the voices of the spirits drifting in desolation around us. He marched with his face set in a grim expression. His quiet determination kept us moving. I wanted to stop, to give in to the cold and just fade. It might not have been the oblivion I once longed for but it offered something close.

When I faltered Hammond pulled me onward and slowly, ever so slowly, the mountain grew larger.

Along the way, we encountered another of the souls who still had the strength to maintain their forms. Once again I tried to communicate with whoever or whatever shadowed us. As with the previous encounter it preferred to keep its distance. I didn't know whether it was the same one as before, but I sensed a deep malevolence from it. It hungered for what little remained of our warmth.

The voices urged me to keep my distance or the thing would consume me as it had so many of them over the centuries. Once it had been human; now it had evolved into so much more. It had become an entity of pure hunger, motivated only by its lust for warmth. The voices might have been eager to talk yet they continued to be reticent to answer questions. I wanted to learn more.

The stalking shape in the dark backed away and faded in the distance. It followed us as we marched — of that I was certain. The voices claimed that others prowled in our wake, hoping for a feast.

I wished I could silence the voices. They weakened my resolve as much as the cold did. All throughout the long journey Hammond bolstered my strength. I wanted to succumb to the chill and he kept me moving.

The spot of white in the black sky didn't change, but the mountain grew larger until — after what seemed like an eternity —

we reached the foot of its slopes. The relief warmed us although only for a short while.

The mountain loomed a monstrous black but there the similarity with the rest of the realm we had seen ended. The mountain formed massive cliffs of razor-edged obsidian which stretched upwards far out of sight.

Its height towered over us yet the pinprick of light remained visible. It hadn't changed in size in all the time we'd walked towards it, almost as if it wasn't a physical object here in the underworld.

Exhausted as we were, the prospect of climbing the mountain wasn't a happy one. I studied the cliff face before us. There appeared to be plenty of handholds so I experimentally climbed a few yards up the cliff.

An angry roar disturbed my concentration and, looking down, I saw the Friar convulsing on the ground and Hammond wrestling with a shadow form. The voices in the air screamed their terror and the weight of it kept me clinging to the black glass — but only for a moment.

I'm not one to back down from a fight so I leapt from the cliff onto the thing struggling with Hammond. It howled as I crushed the being with my falling weight. It rolled away from us then with a single fluid motion it flipped and charged straight back at me.

Its touch chilled me, colder than even the ground which had drained our strength throughout the long trek. I grasped it back; it might have looked like shadow but felt solid to my touch. Its strength matched my own and it took all my effort to hold my grip.

Hammond shouted from behind me. The thing held me in a violent embrace and several seconds passed before I manoeuvred myself to a position where I could see what Hammond faced.

Another shadow form pulled at the Friar, who battled demons within his own mind. The fact that I heard him over the noise from the voices surprised me. Hammond charged the shadow and forced it away from the Friar.

My opponent took advantage of my distraction and pressed its attack. The thing smothered me by changing its form; it still felt solid, but changed shape as easily as smoke.

I understood that I was losing the fight and in desperation I tried to expand my awareness, to attack the thing on another level. It responded by swallowing me in its chill embrace. Enveloped in shadow the cold stunned me. I no longer heard the voices, only my own desperate breathing. The stress had made me slip into my body's memories again.

For minutes I struggled with everything I had, but the effort proved futile. I grew weaker with each passing moment. The shadow seemed content to press against me, smothering my resistance. I'd never been claustrophobic; why would I be with an infinite mind to retreat into? This was different. Its touch covered me, crushing me and piercing deep into my being.

I continued to struggle but failed to establish any grip. I'd almost given up when the creature shuddered in a violent frenzy. I cried out with the sudden force of its constriction, although this seemed somehow different.

One last tremor and then the weight upon me vanished. Still struggling against a foe that was no longer there I crashed to the frozen ground. Cold as it was, it felt warmer than the death grip I'd just escaped.

The Friar stood in front of me, tall and shining with power as he consumed the shadow. He grabbed smoky handfuls of the shaking form and forced them into his mouth. The ferocity of it startled me; the Friar wasn't someone who backed away from a fight either, but he had always fought with a clinical calm.

Piece by piece he tore the thing apart and swallowed the chunks. I was mesmerised by the sight of it until I remembered Hammond and then panicked as I looked around for him. I saw him on the ground at the base of the mountain, struggling with another of the shadow creatures.

I charged over to him and, inspired by the Friar's actions, I gripped a piece of the shadow and ripped it free. The piece felt light and damp, like a sponge in my hand. It took considerable effort to swallow the lump.

It tasted wonderful.

In all my living years I'd never tasted anything so divine. I'd heard that ambrosia was the food of the gods, but I doubt it even came close to that first taste of a soul. I first detected bitterness, like the darkest chocolate layered with the sharp flavour of rage. The taste of another's unsatisfied hunger fuelled my own. The memories of the being's life, followed by a near-eternity in the underworld had aged and enriched the flavours of his spirit.

Eagerly I tore off another smoking chunk from the creature. It screeched in agony as I ripped into its form and gorged upon its strength. I fed in frenzy and didn't stop until Hammond's disgusted face shimmered into focus.

"Stop," he told me.

The energy from the shadow filled me with a high greater than any drug I'd ever indulged in. The Friar too vibrated with energy, although he still looked pale and sick. Only Hammond hadn't fed and he looked more exhausted than ever. The Friar placed his hands on Hammond's shoulders and concentrated. Immediately Hammond looked somewhat restored and together we all turned to face the mountain before us.

Chapter 19
Leap of Faith

The long march across the underworld had been hard, but the climb up the black glass mountain proved even harder. We started well. The energy we'd taken from the shadow creatures renewed our strength and purpose.

We didn't talk as we climbed — we needed all of our focus on finding the next hand or foothold. As before the cold from the stone sucked the strength from our limbs and the sharp edges cut into our hands and feet.

Progress proved slow. Every move up the face took care and deliberation. The fractured glass provided plenty of gaps for us to use. Our angle of ascent meant that the light remained hidden, but even out of sight it wasn't out of mind and all of us sensed its pull, drawing us onward and upward.

I imagine that real climbing takes fitness and well-exercised muscles, but there things worked differently. We no longer had muscles, merely the habit of them. Our ability to move up the cliff came from our will and from our desire to reach the summit, to escape the perpetual gloom of the underworld.

Our arms still hurt from the effort of holding our bodies to the wall. The muscles might no longer be real but we were ingrained with having a body, and it was easier to process the pain in a familiar way.

In truth the climb drained our will. Our legs and arms ached, our hands and feet bled, but it was our very essence that weakened with each movement.

If we hadn't drained those two souls we probably wouldn't have made it. I wanted to stop and rest when we'd climbed high enough that the ground became lost in darkness but Hammond and the Friar urged me to continue. Our grip on the slick surface was precarious at best and we had no way of aiding one another. Beyond vocal support it was an individual effort to reach the top.

The higher we climbed the quieter the voices became and for that I gave small thanks. Their cries and wails of damnation created a constant distraction. For a while I feared they would drive me insane. The fact that this realm lacked physical laws helped us; there were no air currents for the lost souls to float up on.

No wind blew either, which removed another threat from our dangerous climb. The three of us continued to scale the mountain. The only sound was our laboured breathing and frequent curses as new cuts opened in our hands.

I guessed that we reached the halfway point before the light in the sky returned to our view. The sight strengthened our will and renewed our hope, allowing us to ignore our wounds for a little bit longer.

The face remained a sheer slope all the way up. All three of us felt so damn tired. I wanted to rest, even though that would probably kill us. Strange to think of things in those terms even though we'd already died.

I wondered if an afterlife existed beyond the one I already inhabited. I looked down the mountain; it fell away into darkness. What if I fell? The voices claimed there'd be no end, but did that matter?

"Snap to, you fool," Hammond hissed at me. As if waking from a daze I looked at him. His muscles strained as he held position as close to me as he dared. It took a huge effort to nod at him and pull myself to the next spot.

Hammond kept close to me as I climbed, chivvying me along when I faltered. The blood on my hands and feet made the glass slippery, requiring ever more concentration to make the next move. I had no idea what Hammond imagined he could do if I stopped or, even worse, fell.

It came as a surprise when we reached the summit. The cliff angled outward, obscuring our view and making the ascent even more difficult. The Friar reached upward but failed to find another foothold and slipped without warning, just catching himself in time.

"We're there." He grunted as he pulled himself over the ledge.

Several minutes later, Hammond pulled himself over and then he and the Friar pulled me up after them. The top of the mountain appeared flat, like a small plateau. We lay on the smooth stone glass and it chilled our backs, but we were too relieved to have made it to notice. My arms and legs trembled so much I thought I was having a fit.

The chill eventually brought us back to our senses and we wearily stood and faced the light that had beckoned us here. My first instincts had been correct: this wasn't a light where none other existed. Here we saw a doorway, a hole in the sky.

And through it I saw Hemal.

To say I was surprised would have been an understatement. She looked exactly as she had the first time we'd met and she'd worn her sexy human skin.

"Help us," I shouted at her.

"I can't," she shouted back. "I cannot enter. The ward they placed on me prevents my entry and it's taking all of my strength just to hold this portal open."

I looked across as the person-sized hole that hung in the air.

"You need to jump across, all of you."

I measured the gap. The portal hung over a drop all the way to the bottom of the mountain. It would be a long and final fall if I jumped and missed. Smashed to pieces, I'd haunt this realm of the damned for eternity. That didn't sound so bad, but the idea of failure did.

Yes, pride remained my greatest sin.

The distance looked to be only a few yards, yet as exhausted as we were it might as well have been twice as far.

"Hurry," Hemal urged.

The Friar jumped first. With only a few strides to propel him he leapt into the air and through the portal. Hemal caught him and helped him to his feet.

Hammond jumped next; he was the most tired of us all and stumbled as he sprang off the mountain. I saw the panic flash across his face as he realised he might not make it. His tall frame saved him, but only just. He reached the portal and started to slip out, so the Friar and Hemal grabbed his arms and pulled him through.

Then came my turn.

I took a deep and calming breath. I told myself I only had to jump a few metres and I'd be able to do that. With my feet slick with blood, I made sure to clean them before trying. Another deep breath (I didn't need to breathe, so why did I?) and I ran. My feet pounded the glass, reopening the wounds, and on the last step I slipped as I'd seen Hammond do.

Unfortunately I lacked Hammond's height. Even as I stretched out I realised that I wouldn't reach the portal. One of those strange frozen moments occurred. Everything took place in slow motion and I fell. I plummeted from the sky with my own screams filling my ears.

In a panic I stretched out trying to grasp that edge of salvation.

Impossibly my hands touched the portal.

It couldn't happen. I was falling, beyond reach and yet my hands gripped the edge and with a huge effort I pulled myself through the portal.

Chapter 20
Back in the Tunnels

To be back in the light, even the alien pallid light of the tunnel walls, felt amazing. We'd been in the dark for so long that it took a few minutes to adjust. It didn't matter; simply being in the light again had restored us. I lay against the cool resin and closed my eyes, bathing in the warmth. Hemal talked in a rush; so did Hammond and the Friar. If I concentrated then I'm sure I might have understood the words they spoke, but to be honest the light upon my face counted for so much more in that moment.

Everything else could wait, even if only for a few minutes.

I allowed my mind to wander while they babbled around me like a forest brook. Now there was a pleasant image. I'd not been one for nature since an early age, but the image of a vibrant forest scene flashed in my mind and I revelled in the tranquillity of it.

Since my passing I'd found it all too easy to lose myself — although rarely in anything of significance — and that concerned me. Over the years I'd developed the talent of searching within myself, and hiding there if I needed to. These trances seemed different; they lacked purpose. My mind just wandered, oblivious of any concern. I liked them; the sensation of floating was a pleasant one, and when I drifted I experienced no pain or worry.

I think I could have happily lost myself there forever.

Hemal's musical voice brought me back. I didn't want to return, but she insisted. Her face filled my vision once I returned. Her ethereal beauty had come back, a little pale for my tastes, but she still stirred me in a way I hadn't experienced since passing over.

I wondered what sex with an angel would be like and stopped as she scowled down at me. I shrugged. If she didn't like what was in my head then she should keep out of it. I doubted that I'd have the required stamina anyway.

"Now sleeping beauty has returned to us we have much to do."

I sat up. "Where have you been?"

"I returned to Eden to look for allies. You can't imagine how bad it is up there now." "Can we still achieve our goal?" Hammond asked.

"I believe so. As well as the fortunes of the war I spoke to an old friend and he told me of Belial."

"Belial? He's a powerful demon," the Friar commented.

"You need to forget your learning, Friar," Hemal told him. "Belial is no demon. Belial is an archangel from an early founding. Not the first, but he still stands as one of the most powerful."

"How so?" I asked.

"During the extermination of the demons, all angels were charged with destroying demonkind wherever they hid. We obeyed the command; well all of us except one."

"Belial," I guessed.

"Yes. He fought, but he didn't kill the demons — he consumed them instead."

"That was possible?"

"Apparently, or so I am told. No other angel tried, but Belial did."

"Did Michael and Lucifer not condemn this?"

"They might have done if they'd known, but by the time his deeds were discovered he had grown strong. So strong that only the great archangels had the power to challenge him directly."

"Why didn't they?"

"Belial took no sides, and unlike the other archangels he possessed no armies. He kept out of the politics and dwelt with just a few followers on the outskirts of Hell. My friend didn't know for sure, but he suspects that he made a deal with Lucifer."

"How does this help us?"

"I'm hoping that consuming the demons imparted some knowledge of their kind."

I remembered my mind soaking up Lazarus' memories when I consumed the miracle from him, so the idea didn't seem so farfetched to me. Besides I'd seen stranger things.

"Ok, so we track down Belial and find out what he knows."

"How will we find him?" the ever-practical Hammond asked.

"That shouldn't be too difficult; he built a tower on the far reaches. It should be easy to find."

"Why will he help us?" A pertinent question, I thought.

"We'll have to figure it out. I tried a few other sources but didn't find out anything useful. He has a reputation for keeping out of everything and as such there's not much information, or even gossip to learn anything from."

"First we have to get to him. How do we get to Hell?"

"That's easy — we follow the tunnels."

Chapter 21
Road to Hell

The walk through the tunnels proved far less wearying than the march through the underworld. At least the floor didn't drain our essence when we rested. Unlike the first tunnel we'd entered this formed a part of a network; scratch that, it was a maze.

"Wouldn't it be easier to travel across the surface?" I asked while we rested in the pallid green light.

"I have the ability to travel there in an instant," Hemal replied. "Unfortunately you are bound to your bodies so we have to follow the same methods that you are familiar with, which means walking through the tunnels."

We soon lost our sense of direction as we passed through junctions and different tunnels. We encountered no landmarks, no way of knowing one passageway from another. At our next rest stop I asked Hemal more about the tunnels, and why they led to Hell.

"They were built for trade. Many souls were surprised to learn that Hell wasn't the inferno they'd been told. Many angels in Hell were happy to deal with humans, even if they couldn't do so officially."

"Contact with humans was controlled?"

"You know part of the story already. At first humans seemed no more than a novelty. They were God's creation and kept apart from Heaven and Hell. Lucifer was first to realise your potential. His armies had always been outnumbered by Michael's loyalists, so he wanted your kind to bolster his forces. Lucifer decided that only his recruiters should contact human souls in Eden and bring them into the fold."

"I take it not everyone agreed."

"No. Lucifer has never had the same level of control over his forces that Michael does. It does have its advantages; they tend to be more innovative than the loyalists, but also play their own games."

"Hence the tunnels?"

"Yes, although humans can only form themselves into tunnels or other constructions for that matter in Eden."

"Really? Why?"

"I'm not sure. I think it's because Eden was created specifically for humans. Heaven and Hell are God's pure essence; humans haven't developed themselves enough to manipulate his essence."

The answer didn't satisfy my curiosity. Sure, I could see why God would give us Eden as a playground to learn how to play with our new toys, but hearing that no-one had ever mastered the big boy toys seemed a little unlikely. Still it wasn't important for now so I let it slide and filed it away for a later conversation.

"All right, so if humans can't build tunnels into Hell how close do they go?"

"All the way. Where humans lacked the ability to build, some of the enterprising fallen did. We can get all the way into Hell through the tunnels."

"What about Belial's domain?"

"We'll need to cross through Hell to get there."

"Wonderful. Won't you stand out a bit there?"

"Not as much as you will."

"Fair enough — now why are these tunnels such a maze?"

"That I don't know."

Conversation drifted after that and for a while we slept, with Hemal keeping guard. I dreamt when I slept, but it seemed different. I'd always been a lucid dreamer; you don't spend as much time inside your own head as I had over the years without learning how to control your thoughts.

I dreamed of the lives I didn't live, the choices I hadn't made. In each instant I existed with all the possibilities of what I might have been. It taunted me with the realisation that the world would have been different if I had not been the person I chose to be.

I never had time for regret, and even locked in that odd dream state I had no intention of starting to lose myself in such thoughts. Yet a part of me did reach out for that alien emotion and wanted to wallow in it.

The stronger part, the one which had made the choices, wondered where the dream had come from; did the traitorous part of me create it? Or something from outside? Or the real me? Whatever that meant.

I wanted to focus on those questions more, but the blur of trillions of lives seized my attention and drowned it with more than I could ever hope to understand. I cursed my own mind for even trying to comprehend the impossibility of what I saw.

The dream locked me in its grip until Hammond shook me awake, still exhausted.

"Are you ok?"

I shook my head. I felt far from ok.

Hammond helped me stand.

"We have to move on."

Time passed and we continued through the maze, stopping to rest when we grew weary. When I slept the dream returned and it remained the same every time — actually that wasn't true, but the changes each time appeared so slight it took a while for me to notice.

The same overwhelming multitude of all my lives not lived returned. And you know what? I became used to it. At first confusion dominated, until gradually I mastered the streams. I learned how to pick and choose at will. The flow of it remained beyond my control, but the detail of it became mine to choose.

In a sense I started to enjoy the dream — the temptation of regret lurking beneath the memories of all those lives. I considered there was a lesson somewhere, although one I couldn't fathom.

The gaps between the rests grew shorter and the lack of real rest drained my strength more and more. Hemal and the others tried to help by channelling their own strength into me. It worked for a few stops, but the empty expanse inside me wasn't so easily filled.

More than that I came to prefer the dream world, in which I was everything that I wanted to be. In those infinite lives I possessed strength and power. This wouldn't be the first time I'd been seduced by escaping into fantasy. The years spent exploring drugs had been the first occasion.

This time felt different. Then I'd maintained a level of control; now I let myself slip deeper and ignored the concern of those around me. I let them carry me and allowed myself to drown in my unlived lives.

Strangely I received no comfort. Sure, it provided escape — but not in a way which bolstered me. Outside of my mind the others kept moving; I lost track of the direction and, in truth, I didn't care.

I'd met a few smackheads during my experimentation days. When they tried quitting they used methadone to help them along the way. It didn't give you the high like the real thing, but it dulled the misery of their existence.

Watching those other lives helped me in the same way. I understood from my conversations with Venet (the bastard) and Hemal how the transformation shocked souls passing through it.

I considered my reaction at the time. I'd labelled those souls as weak minds and here I slumped, falling apart. So much had happened since passing over, yet that alone didn't explain my collapse. The shame of it stung me — not enough to break me out of the funk, but enough for me to start digging.

The mind is a wonderful thing. It can be directed by conscious thought, but also creates ideas of its own volition. My mind had always possessed its own peculiar bent. I'd never been averse to a little introspection, but this time proved something very different.

Maybe the transformation had changed me, but that didn't sit right. While the dream snared me in its grasp I examined it closer. I sensed a pattern that I couldn't discern clearly, and also wondered where the dream had come from.

Over and over again I watched the web of lives play out. I lived them as if they replaced the one I'd just lost; it wasn't at all like watching a biography. That's when the realisation dawned.

None of these lives were my own. In all of the millions of lives and combinations of choices none of them resembled the life I'd actually lived.

With that understanding I knew that someone (or something) had to be interfering with me. I wondered who and why. I'd find no answers in this dream — I needed to return. It didn't prove as easy as slipping into the dream's clutches had been.

Layer upon layer of deception befuddled my mind, and I tore through them as if wading through masses of spider webs. Each layer offered no real resistance, but together they slowed my progress.

Before, the lives of the not-me's provided a distraction; now they resisted. They infected my thoughts with their presence. I found it hard to distinguish between my real memories and the fake ones.

I waded through each fake existence, the surge of my initial anger at the deception fading. My progress slowed with my diminished will, although I didn't give up; the idea that I almost had offended me. That might not sound like much motivation, but as I've said before I've always been a prideful creature.

Sheer strength alone wouldn't enable me to free myself from this trap. The weight of all those realities seemed too much. I had to think of a different approach. My mind was always my own domain; it needed to become so again.

I retreated into a bubble I created, a black sphere of nothing with my core at the centre. The surface sparked as the invading thoughts assaulted the shield. It required considerable effort to maintain the barrier, but less than my previous direct attack and it gave me the time I needed to think.

Chapter 22
Weathering the Storm

I remained in the calm centre I'd created amidst the maelstrom of confusion. I examined what little I'd discovered about the trap and it convinced me this was a deliberate attempt to keep me out of the game. The why seemed simple enough — it had to be one of Lucifer's minions trying to prevent me from disrupting their master's plan.

Perhaps that bastard Venet? A pleasant thought to be sure. I'd have loved another crack at him. His deception had led ultimately to my demise by the Antichrist's hand.

That memory led to another pleasant one. If they were trying to stop me then our plan had some merit. Not that I didn't trust Hemal; well I didn't, not really. I'd always had trust issues. There's only one person you can trust in life, or the next one for that matter.

My interaction with the Friar and Hammond had changed my viewpoint a little. Not enough to change a lifetime of learning, but enough to give it a second thought.

I'd had my doubts since being told I had to speak directly to God. The familiar question of 'why me?' had occurred to me more than once. Since being introduced to the world beyond the physical universe I'd encountered some strange things and been tasked with even harder challenges.

None of those challenges even came close to trying to fix the current mess. Of course it was academic if I didn't escape the dream and it sure didn't want to let me leave.

This was my mind, though — and that had to give me some advantage. The dream didn't allow me to withdraw from its advances for long. It swamped my barrier, which sparked like a fireworks display under the onslaught.

The pressure mounted as more and more lives piled upon my shield. I held it off for a while, but I wouldn't be able keep it up for long. Brute force had failed me. There had to be some other way out of this.

I cast out a lance of my will through the shield to determine if I remained locked in my body. It speared through the assaulting layers with ease and, as expected, encountered the barrier around my body.

So whoever caused the attacks had found a way through, which meant I might find a way out — or so I hoped. It also raised the chance that the others could help if I found some way of communicating with them.

I didn't like the thought. It implied that I couldn't solve the problem for myself. I'd never been one to rely on others. Again, recent events had tempered that outlook a bit, but not so much that I liked the idea.

The pressure on my shield continued to build, and soon it took too much effort to hold it back. I let it collapse and once again I danced in the maelstrom. For a moment I tried to control my movement through the flow but realised that it was futile.

I let myself go.

The lives that weren't mine washed through me, tempting me with their differences. There lay the key to the puzzle. It hovered just out of reach and when I tried to grasp it another phantom life intruded.

The truth that I no longer controlled my own mind frightened me.

I'd always processed fear into rage, externalising it, and I followed that path again. Fire scorched through the lives which threatened to consume me, much like the miracle's fire had once seared my flesh.

The dream hadn't been prepared for my counterattack, which blazed through its constructs. It recoiled and then surged in response. Instead of fighting it I let it carry me upon its eddies, all the while unleashing my hot anger. It glowed brighter than any sun.

My rage was finite, unlike the great flood of lives which filled the void I'd created. I soon tired and the tsunami flowed back in. I remembered how I managed to enter Hammond's mind without the ability to leave my own. It would be a slim chance, but I took it anyway — better to act and be wrong than, well, than to do nothing at all.

With a huge effort I roared my defiance in a glowing fireball which incinerated all that it touched. I kept all that mattered to me safe in the core of my being. As the fire expanded out I blinked and collapsed back into the previous moment.

I reached into the moment and summoned my strength and unleashed another fireball as I released the first one. Another blink and I slipped back again to an earlier moment, created another tempest and cast it forth with the first and second.

Again and again I repeated the process, and kept doing so until it became too much effort to return to an earlier moment. With that done I returned to the present and watched the fire tear through the far reaches of my mind with the force of a nuclear explosion.

The bright light filled my vision, blinding me from the inside out. The dream had bombarded my sense for too long and shredded it into nothing. After the roar of the detonation faded I was blessed with silence.

Not for long, but at least these new voices sounded more familiar. The light lessened too, resolving into the pale green glow of the tunnels and my friends.

Yes, the realisation surprised me too, but the relief at seeing the Friar and especially Hammond (he acted like a loyal puppy!) in the flesh again overwhelmed me with emotions I'd never expected to experience again.

It was a tender moment to be sure.

They looked pleased to see me too, and their joy sparked another surge. I swallowed it back down where it belonged. After a barrage of questions I told them about the dream, my escape and about my suspicions.

Hemal appeared perplexed.

"I've never heard of anything like this."

"Nothing at all?" Her comment seemed odd to me as I'd caused very similar tricks back in the world.

She understood what I meant.

"Things work differently here; there is no separation between mind and body. In truth there isn't back in your world, not at the most fundamental level, but the way your minds work insist that you do."

Her answer didn't satisfy me because, of all people, I knew how intrinsically tied mind and body were. I didn't think she was trying to deceive me, but something felt wrong.

"How does that prevent what I experienced?"

"It doesn't, but it makes it unlikely." She stopped for a few seconds before continuing. "When the soul is born filled with your life, a transformation occurs. This change removes the illusions of separation, but the human mind is an unusual construct.

"Angels are beings of pure energy, if you like. We change our forms at will to suit our mood or purpose. It's also good practice for when we visit the physical realm. Remember, the physical universe is only a small part of the totality of creation."

"I get that, but what does it mean for us?"

"Usually the transformation opens possibilities for the soul, but certain habits, like the form of your body, are so indelibly imprinted in your psyche they can't be changed."

"I still don't see how that affects how my abilities work."

"Your abilities are simply your mental capacity to change the physical order of things which means that you're better able to fit into how things work here in the celestial realm."

"So why don't my abilities work here?"

"That's what's odd. You should be more able than most and I don't understand why."

"Who would know?"

"Again, I'm not sure, but I believe there's a similarity with the entity that we seek."

Now that statement intrigued me; it opened a wealth of possibilities.

"You're suggesting I have something in common with the true demons?"

The Friar and Hammond both looked surprised at this suggestion.

Hemal nodded.

"I'm not sure. It does sound far-fetched when you say it out loud. However, their weakness was their inability to interact directly with creation. They were sealed off from creation in some way. I can't say for certain if it's the same as what you're experiencing, but it's the only similar situation I'm aware of.

"Perhaps Belial would know more."

I hoped that he would. I wanted to understand the events unfolding. Another failing of mine — I hated not understanding things, especially if I happened to be in the centre of it.

"Well, let's find him."

Hammond spoke then.

"We have a problem there."

Wonderful.

"What kind of problem?"

"We seem to be lost."

Before I responded a terrible shriek echoed through the tunnel.

Chapter 23
Hunted

Now we were lost and hunted. The shrieking came from the same direction in which we were headed. Being lost could be put off until later; first we had to head away from the horrible noise.

There's a saying that it takes one to know one. I knew the sound of a predator, and this wasn't one who hunted for food. I recognised the call of a special type of beast which hunted for sadistic pleasure — much as I had done, although in fairness I tended to be a bit more circumspect about it.

From what Hemal had told us, these creatures didn't hunt alone, although so far we'd only heard a single voice. I considered the option of reversing the tables, tracking down the thing that had once been human and silencing it.

Without my usual abilities I didn't feel as confident that I could kill the shrieking thing, but the four of us together should probably be able to defeat it. I knew Hemal's power was great, but I had no real knowledge of what we would be up against.

So we ran.

I'd never thought of running as a good response to anything, but I had learned a little caution from recent experiences.

It seemed that not only the physical universe liked a sense of the dramatic; the howl of the shrieker chased after us. It sounded a little louder this time. We all glanced back down the corridor.

How was it tracking us?

Hemal guessed my unspoken question.

"It's following our scent."

I didn't even realise we had a scent.

She smiled.

"Of course you don't have a scent in the same way as back in the world, but you do leave a trail of your essence as you move, so it's similar enough."

"Are you reading my mind?"

"No, but you are being a little obvious."

Seeing her humour return pleased me.

"Can you detect our scents?" I asked her.

"Yes."

"Are there any other trails we could follow? Maybe they would lead us out of here."

"Nothing. The trail fades quickly."

Damn.

"Then let's go on the offensive," Hammond suggested.

"I considered that earlier, but these things don't hunt alone. Right?"

I glanced at Hemal for confirmation. She nodded. "That's what I've been told. They're supposed to live in clans down here, but I've never interacted with them before. An angel would easily escape them unless badly injured or surprised."

"But you're not really sure," he insisted.

I faded from the conversation as they discussed their chances of taking the offensive against the thing stalking us. His nature meant this was Hammond's preferred response and I didn't disagree. My idea about the trails buzzed around my head looking for somewhere to settle.

Not being able to expand my awareness beyond the confines of my body also hindered my thinking. I'd become used to casting out my thoughts to explore situations and ideas, but with my thoughts trapped inside me the solution proved so much more difficult to reach.

Still, this old dog was capable of learning some new tricks, or at least adapting some old ones. I summoned the memory of the tunnel we followed and within the freedom of my mind I searched for trails. I noticed ours immediately.

When the idea surfaced I'd imagined the lines of scent as an ethereal trail, something like a comet's tail. What I saw appeared more complicated. It did form a trail; however it matched the shape and volume we had occupied for that instant.

I scanned along the trail and it reminded me of the flick book animations I'd drawn as a child, when bored at school. Three-dimensional shapes of us formed an infinite array of translucent statues back down the corridor from where we came.

At a glance I saw every moment as a continual line, time's arrow laid out in all its glory — interesting to be sure, but I'm not sure what it gained me.

Insight.

It hovered, bugging my conscious thoughts, like someone waving in the distance trying to attract my attention. I followed our trail back down the tunnel and back through time. My control lacked finesse at first — digital rather than the analogue of fine control.

I located another trail at a junction not far from where I recovered from the dream assault. This trace was so faint that I almost missed it. The form appeared little more than shadow across the dimly lit floor.

Unfortunately I had no way of estimating how long the trail had been there. It looked so dim that I guessed it might have been years, perhaps more. I deduced the direction of travel from the vague form of the trails and with no other option I followed it.

The trail led me on and on through the maze, which I hoped would lead me somewhere useful. Along the way I encountered other trails which appeared tinged with red. They vibrated with such rage that I assumed them to be the shriekers. I considered following one, to learn more about them, but that information wouldn't get us out of here.

I experienced an odd feeling following the trail through the passages. My instinct told me that this had to be the right way, but one thought gave me pause. If I did find a way out, how would I remember the path to take?

I already had the answer, I just didn't realise it then — or rather I didn't bother investigating it. The problem bothered me for a while, so I stopped to think about it. The trail was there, a little bit more distinct than when I first spotted it, but not by much.

I noticed that I didn't see any trail for myself. It made sense, of course; I travelled through my own memory. Except that I had never been this far into the tunnels, so how could I see the layout I shouldn't have known? It's possible I imagined it, but that didn't seem right.

So, if the layout was already in my memory I wouldn't have to remember it; I already did.

With that soothing thought I continued my quest, I'd also realised that time didn't pass here in my head. I might have lost the ability to exert control beyond my body, but within it I had complete control.

Which felt amazing.

I would have swapped it for my old abilities. I didn't feel complete without them, but it helped a little.

My realisation of control sped up the search. Before, I'd followed the trail as if walking along the tunnel. There was no need to limit myself in that fashion — what had Hemal said? Ah yes, an angel simply had to picture their destination and there they would appear. Inside my own head I should be able to do the same, so I did.

Only a brief moment had passed for the others. They were still arguing when I opened my eyes.

"I know the way out."

They didn't hear me at first, or maybe they preferred to argue about whether they should take the fight to the shrieker hunting us. I repeated myself and this time Hemal heard me and gave me a quizzical look.

"How do you know?"

I responded with what I hoped was a beatific smile.

"I have seen the way."

Chapter 24
Pandemonium

We had to walk out the old-fashioned way. I really wanted to understand why we were confined to the memories of our bodies in this manner — and in particular why I couldn't extend my will beyond its confines. It seemed strange that in all the history of humanity no soul had ever broken their prison of flesh.

The shrieks still followed us along the way, but they always sounded far in the distance. We followed the trail which I'd found until eventually we reached the surface and into Hell.

The brief glimpse I'd seen when I stole Lazarus' miracle gave me some indication of what to expect, but the reality of it proved so much more. Hell lacked the boiling lakes reeking of sulphur from the classic stories of literature — although considering the individual nature of the structures within it, I guessed that there might be such a scene somewhere. It didn't have the coherent wonder of Heaven, yet still provided a scene to capture the eye and the imagination.

An abundance of shapes and structures formed Hell. Some showed human artistic and architectural influences. It reminded me of what you see in ancient cities: a clash of styles which somehow blends into a harmonious whole.

Well, perhaps not that harmonious, but it looked impressive all the same. The sheer craft and ingenuity of the spectacle around us stunned me. This was more than architecture. Some of the buildings looked as if they'd been constructed in a familiar manner; most however did not.

The first building to catch my eye looked like a giant wave frozen in time and placed in this city. 'City' fitted as a human concept, but the term didn't do the sight justice. A city implies a large population compressed into a small area, but nothing looked squeezed-in here.

The structures came in all shapes and sizes. They towered above us, but between the constructs we saw vast open spaces. Each building had a different form, and the variety stretched to the horizon and I suspected beyond my sight as well.

The landscape between the buildings was as varied as the buildings it surrounded. Tempests of water danced in wide circles around the frozen wave. Not only elements filled our vision, strange mysteries of colour, shape and light dazzled our minds.

The frozen wave was one of the more comprehensible sights of this scene, which made my eyes hurt to behold. Most of the objects in view appeared to be little more than impossible geometries which formed no discernible shape, or at least none that my mind found familiar.

At first glance the city had looked like a human city — a flat plane covered in a web of buildings. As my eyes (or more accurately my mind) adjusted I caught the truth of the reality I perceived.

The city appeared to be constructed from an infinite number of planes which intersected at a multitude of angles and distances. I'd experienced something similar in the deepest acid trips of my youth: a world too complex for my mind to fully grasp, but then it had been the network of social interactions surrounding me.

My mind's ability to enter and track the minds of others allowed me to map the connections between people. The connections formed a many-layered map of friendships, emotional connections and social interactions. That had been a complex web of no more than a hundred or so people.

What I saw now stretched way beyond my small microcosm of humanity. Here I beheld a construct of millions of the fallen. Each of the buildings represented the personal domain of one of the fallen, built in the image of their desire and will.

Again I remembered the tantalising images from Lazarus' mind. The difference between this city of the fallen and majesty of

Heaven appeared stark — not in the quality of the constructions, but the individuality, the breadth of the imagination which populated Hell. It almost seemed strange to call it Hell. After all, the baggage that came with the name seemed inappropriate.

We saw no sky here. In every direction the domains filled our vision. The structures folded and twisted through each other, adding the chaos of confusion to my vision of the stunning architecture.

For a moment I struggled to comprehend what I saw, so much so that a wave of nausea crashed through my body. I looked down at my feet to centre myself and after a few seconds the sickness faded.

In the instant when my confusion passed I learned a new lesson. There was more here than I realised; the sheer scale of it was too much for me to understand. I'm quite used to bulling my way through the problem. My usual tactic wouldn't work here just like it hadn't helped within the dream.

Sometimes you have to roll with the flow and let understanding seep in slowly. I looked at the Friar and Hammond and saw that they too experienced sensory overload from the world around us. Only Hemal accepted the scene with equanimity. That shouldn't have been a surprise; after all her kind had built this place.

"Why are we seeing this now? Why didn't we see it in Eden or in the tunnels?"

"You did see it in Eden, although not in Eden itself — you saw it in me." She was right, I remembered seeing the infinite impossibilities through the tears in her human skin. "God created Eden to allow human souls to adapt to the transition. In the physical universe the impossible is generally invisible or ignored. Those options don't work as well here. Everything which is can be seen."

"I guess our minds try to disguise what they are seeing by using familiar constructs," the Friar commented. Hammond also seemed to have recovered from the shock of seeing Hell for the first time.

"That's correct," Hemal replied.

"And why not in the tunnels?" I asked.

"They are human constructs; like your bodies they follow a form which is familiar to you."

I accepted her explanation, in part because the place seemed to be deserted — which was even more of a surprise than the complexity.

"Where is everyone?" I asked Hemal.

"The war."

"Everyone?"

I didn't believe it.

"We need no logistics and angels can travel instantly. I'm sure there are a few watchers scattered about, but the only real threat would come from Michael's forces and they're all bogged down on the borders of Eden."

"Why don't they just transport themselves here?"

"Michael's forces? To what purpose? They would destroy some of Hell and in return Lucifer would destroy parts of Heaven. In either case no advantage would be gained. Humanity is the real threat — one that both sides are near to destroying forever."

"But everyone? That doesn't make sense."

"It makes perfect sense. Lucifer doesn't want Hell; he wants all of creation. Michael may have helped provide the power needed to bring Earth into this realm, but Lucifer destroyed the Earth where he wanted it, right behind the front lines where Michael's forces were engaged with the human rebels. "How much time do we have?"

She shrugged, "I don't know, but we shouldn't waste time admiring the sights."

"Well, let's get moving then." I pointed through the carefully-crafted chaos into the distance. "We need to head that way."

Hemal looked surprised. "How do you know that?"

She asked a fair question, one I didn't have a clear answer for. I hadn't delved into myself to explore my mind's creation of my surroundings. To be honest I feared to do so. How would my mind reconstruct the vast and twisted reality of what I saw before me? I didn't comprehend it correctly with my usual senses, and relying on ones which didn't work as they once did represented a step beyond what I was willing to cross.

The silence lengthened between us. Hammond intervened and said, "We'd better get moving then."

We did have a long way to go. If my sense proved correct then Belial's domain was on the far side of Hell.

Chapter 25
Audience

We passed through Hell more quickly than we had through the tunnels, in part because we could follow a more direct path. I think that being under an open sky upped our pace. Hell's empty atmosphere also added urgency to our trek. I knew how far we had to travel; however, the distance we covered didn't match the footsteps we planted. Another puzzle to add to the constant barrage I'd experienced since passing over.

I hadn't enjoyed passing over. Sure, I'd learned a few new things, but the afterlife had diminished me. In the physical universe I encountered few people who matched my abilities. Here my body imprisoned my will in a manner that weakened me, but I admit that the world inside me had grown in a way I hadn't anticipated.

I'd once dreamed of oblivion, the complete nullification of my existence. In the darkest pits of despair I'd even yearned never to have existed at all. They say that selfishness is the prime cause of evil — reflecting on my life that seemed a fair assessment — but the world had seen many evil people. Were they all changed in the same way as me when they passed over?

I doubted it. It may have been my all too familiar pride talking, but I believed that what I experienced was something unique for me.

But why?

As we walked I pondered these questions and more. The others followed me and talked about the history of creation. Every so often I caught snatches of their conversation. I'd already learned many of the stories that the Friar and Hammond listened to. My conversations in the Parisian cafe by the abyss had informed me of the true history of everything.

Not that it really mattered — and so I wrestled with the things I didn't know.

We encountered nobody during that long walk, although on occasion I did sense that we were being watched. The others admitted to the same sensation. For the first few times we searched the surrounding environment trying to locate the observer, but always without success.

Despite the length of the walk we didn't stop for rest as often as we had in the tunnels. We no longer felt the need. I missed eating and drinking, although hunger and thirst didn't bother me. We regenerated energy simply by being, drawing what we needed from the air around us. Not that we breathed; it seemed more like a process of osmosis.

I slept on the few instances we stopped, although the others remained awake. Apparently no-one in the afterlife required or even desired sleep. My dreams were filled with the structural wonders which we'd seen on our journey so far.

The dreams weren't unpleasant, whatever their cause, and I woke refreshed when one of the others roused me. We continued our journey with little conversation. I realised that the dreams confused Hemal, who had never seen anything like it. She disliked not understanding a puzzle as much as I did.

The confusion of interwoven dimensions lessened as we reached the far side of Hell's collective domains. By this point the sight no longer strained my eyes, but it was still agreeable not to have to organise the order of the things I saw. We continued to march until the city flattened into a vast plain of shimmering glass.

The immense field of glass presented a space much larger than any of the other of the domains we had seen on our travels. A solitary tower stood at the centre, barely visible in the distance. It too was formed from the same glass which reflected and refracted a myriad of colours. Its sides appeared smooth and without any ornamentation, a stark difference from what we'd seen before.

We rested for a short time before stepping onto the glass. We didn't need to rest; I think we simply wanted to prepare for what we hoped would be a change in our fortunes. The moment my foot touched the surface everything around us warped with a twisted pinch and blinked out of existence.

Without time for shock or surprise we appeared in a vast chamber made from the same glass we'd seen outside. I assumed we were now somewhere inside the tower. How we'd arrived there became yet another mystery.

To be honest I was becoming sick of them.

The room surrounded us in a perfect circle about a hundred yards in width. Light reflected from all of the surfaces although I didn't see any sources. I saw no furniture or ornamentation, but I did see a being standing opposite us.

He wore a human shape — for our benefit, I guessed — although he clearly wasn't used to wearing it. The general shape looked correct: two arms, two legs and head, but it lacked any recognisable human features. The proportions also appeared wrong, not in any obvious sense apart from his size. More apparent than that was his true essence which boiled with fractal immensity visible beneath his skin.

The interplay of energies hurt my eyes to look at, in the same way the true vision of Hell had done at first. For a minute we all stood in silence measuring each other. The shimmering of power made him look jittery, as if nervous, but in truth he stood absolutely still, his energy warping reality around him. He waited for us to make our move.

I decided to take the initiative.

"Are you Belial?"

"An interesting name. I have never heard it spoken in such simplistic terms."

Ah, a pompous angel; who would have thought it.

"Is it your name?"

"Yes, but who are you to ask me that? Never has your kind visited my domain." He looked at Hemal. "Another oddity. You are very far from home; this is not a good place for you to be."

I glanced at the others, but they appeared content for me to be our spokesman. I'm not sure that was their wisest decision, but I happily spoke for them.

"We're hoping that you can help us."

"Why would I want to help you? Do you comprehend the danger you are in? More than that, do you understand the peril you bring to my domain?"

"Danger is everywhere."

"True, but I see that it follows you like an eager lover." I felt a bit taken aback by his statement; he didn't know me. My thoughts were apparently his to read. "Your past is written in the very fabric of your being. It doesn't matter — it is too late now.

"What does matter is that I have remained in solitude longer than your kind has existed. I appreciate the irony of the fact that I have never hunted your kind and yet now you will be my undoing."

That seemed an odd thing to say. I tried to convince him that we didn't present a threat. He chuckled in response.

"I did not say that you had come to do me harm; I doubt you could if you tried. As I said, danger follows in your wake."

"We need your help."

"You said that already, and what helps is it that you want from me?"

"We're looking for the last true demon."

"What a strange quest. The demons were all purged many eons ago, before your universe came to be. It was the last time all of angel kind worked with a single purpose. In my opinion that was our great fall, not the squabbles beforehand."

"Is that why you didn't destroy them, but consumed them instead?"

"Did she tell you that?" He indicated Hemal. "I suppose it doesn't matter now. Yes, it's true that I didn't destroy the essence of the demons."

"Why not?"

"It didn't seem right, not then and not now."

"Why?"

"They formed part of creation; separate in a way that others didn't understand, but nothing which is part of God should be destroyed."

"I have been told that they weren't part of creation and had to be destroyed, as they posed a threat to Heaven."

"That might have been true, but no-one knew for certain. I tried to convince my brothers and sisters that we shouldn't have purged them, that it wasn't our choice to make."

"I take it nobody listened?"

"Only one and he refused to take part in the purge at all."

"Who was that?"

"Before we get to that, why do you seek the demons? And what makes you think there is one left?"

I told him of the destruction of Earth and of humanity, I also spoke of Lucifer's deception and his plan to conquer creation. When I finished he nodded.

"I have been away from things for a long time. I sympathise with your struggle. I have never feasted upon human souls as many have."

His comment sparked my curiosity. "Why not?"

"As with the demons it didn't seem right. Angels don't need power; we have all we need right here. God created us to help us shape his reality, but the physical universe was something different. He created the universe for his own purpose and I'm certain its purpose wasn't to fuel the war between Michael and Lucifer."

"We were told that if we found the last demon then he would be able to help us communicate with God, and it's our only chance to fix what has been broken."

"That's a bold plan, I'll admit, but there are no more demons. We killed them all and I think God will never forgive us for that."

"I thought that God didn't perceive the demons and that was why they posed a threat to creation."

"For a human you have been told many things. I wonder why that should be."

Belial focused his will upon mine and I felt the brush of it across my body.

"Interesting. You possess great power; more than I would have expected for one of your kind, yet deficient somehow. You are the focus for something. You are following a path for events which I can't quite determine."

This might be very interesting, but it didn't help me with my more immediate issues.

"Did you learn anything about the demons when you consumed them?"

He sighed. The very human mannerism surprised me.

"I've been forced to kill angels to protect my domain and to truly kill an angel you have to consume them. And there is an abundance of power which fills you when you absorb them into yourself. Not only that but you gain the knowledge of their experiences. I imagine it's the same with consuming human souls, but I've never felt the desire to find out.

"With the demons it was very different. There is no obvious influx of power; it was more like absorbing an absolute chill. You do gain strength, though — a power which never seems to fade. That is probably why I've been left alone for so long here in my domain.

"Even stranger was the lack of insight or knowledge gained by the feasting. It tasted like swallowing a void, bereft of anything. However, at the edges I sensed some potential. Perhaps their power came from not from what they were, but from what they could be."

I thought about the transformation and of the dream which had almost trapped me within its infinite possibilities. Maybe a link connected them?

"It occurs to me that there is some synchronicity at work here. You seek a demon to help you converse with God."

"Yes."

"Well, I mentioned earlier there is one other who might help you in your quest."

"And who is that?"

He paused. He might have been an angel but he still had to make a decision whether to trust us or throw us out.

"Metatron. Of all the angels in creation he alone refused to take part in the purge of the demons."

"Ok, but I don't see any special connection?"

It was Hemal who cleared it up for me.

"You know that angels represent a specific aspect of God?"

"Yes."

"Well, Metatron is the Voice of God."

Chapter 26
An Old Friend Returns

"Why the Hell did we not go straight to the voice of God?" I demanded of Hemal. She didn't get the chance to respond.

An explosion shattered the glass walls around us, blasting the fragments outwards. Amidst the thunder of the detonation other sounds rang, like musical bells. They grew in volume over the space of seconds until a blinding light drove us to our knees.

"What the fuck?"

I addressed my question to anyone who would listen, not that anyone could. I saw only the complicated white light. The glass floor pressed warm against my face, although moments before it had been cool.

I climbed to my feet as the tolls faded. My sight might still be lost to the light, but I believed in facing anything on my feet rather than cowering on the floor. I recognised great power in the air around us. Naturally I tried to cast my will around me to see who or what had arrived.

My attempt failed, but then I remembered that I controlled that which lay within me so used my will to clear my eyes. I saw again and felt stronger for it. Belial still stood opposite me. He had lost his human shape and now towered like a million pyramids, all glowing and twisting within each other. The geometric perfection stole my breath away.

My friends climbed to their feet behind me. Six angels stood in an arc around us, where the glass walls once circled. All showed their natural form — perfect shapes twisting in glorious energies and complicated clarity.

All glowed with such power that I might have been staring at six suns. Only one of them had a brightness that matched — no, exceeded Belial's energy. Compared to their starlight, he shone greater than an entire universe. I recognised him at once, even though we had never met. In legend he had been known as the Morning Star, once the greatest of the archangels.

Lucifer himself stood before me.

I was drawn to his power like a moth to a flame, although oddly I felt no fear, only wonder.

Here I beheld a being whose strength summed greater than all the galaxies in the universe.

Then a smaller shape snagged my attention; this one wore a human form. No, I realised my mistake, it didn't wear a human skin — it was human. The man had a face I recognised, one I had battled before.

Lazarus.

In an abstract way I had known he still existed, but in all the excitement since my death I'd forgotten that fact. We'd tangled on a few occasions, but now he shone with such power that I flinched from his gaze.

Hard as it is to admit it, that cold look filled me with a fear I hadn't known since the first time I'd encountered him. On that occasion I had escaped only thanks to the Friar and his black-clad commandoes. He looked happy to see me, his smile so broad I thought it would swallow everything around him.

His eyes transfixed me.

If the eyes are windows of the soul, what are they when you look *at* a soul?

In Lazarus' eyes I recognised the same power which fuelled the surrounding angels. On the surface he looked human in every respect, except for the eyes — eyes that now looked upon me with hungry violence.

We were little more than a sideshow; the title match was Lucifer and Belial. Lucifer's voice rang with a pure tone which vibrated through all of us. I didn't hear the voice of evil, or even seductive lies — this was the voice of a leader, strong and true. Even though he wasn't speaking to me I nearly surrendered to a compulsion to bend to his will.

"You have broken our agreement."

"I have broken nothing."

"Then what are these trespassers doing here?" Lucifer's gaze swept across us. I held my ground and stared back into the volcano. "Three humans and one of Michael's host. What do they want?"

I stepped forward.

Think of the arrogance of it, the pride which gave me the strength to step forward and stare into the maelstrom. Unfortunately for me the Prince of Hell didn't think much of it.

"I know who you are, human." Thanks for the validation! "I was present in the moment when my son tore immortality from your body. Without you my plan would have been more difficult to realise. For your help I have a special reward."

"That's very generous, but I don't think you have anything I want."

I'm pretty good at presenting a strong front, but in the face of Lucifer's magnificence it took all my effort to keep my voice level.

"I have an old friend of yours who is eager to reminisce about old times, but for now you are of no significance. It is my old friend Belial who I'm here to see."

His shimmering form flashed at me as I opened my mouth to speak again. It was one of the few occasions in my life when I took the hint.

"Now that the insect has stopped buzzing, how about you tell me what this little group wanted?"

Belial remained silent.

"I suppose it doesn't matter. I already know exactly what these four want, which is why I've watched them travelling across my realm. For your sake I hoped they wouldn't reach your tower, but knowing what it is they wanted it didn't surprise me when they ended up here."

Still no response from Belial.

"I know precisely what this little group want with you. They want to speak to the ghosts inside of you."

"There are no ghosts. They died."

"You think I believe that? I let you live here under my protection just in case what is inside you ever became useful. Regrettably the time has come where they pose a threat, so I'm afraid our deal is done."

Belial made the first move. He realised that talking only delayed the inevitable; maybe taking the initiative would give him the edge. He faced a superior enemy, not only in strength but in numbers. Lucifer presented the main threat which is why he surprised me by launching his attack against all of them except Lazarus — but he probably didn't consider Lazarus a threat.

Four lances of the brightest energy speared across the room from Belial. Each one struck Lucifer and his escorts. The lesser angels crumbled under the onslaught. Lucifer paused only for a brief moment before responding with his own power.

The sight mesmerised me. I watched two suns battle each other. Titanic flashes blazed wherever they touched each other. A storm of reflected energy filled the room with sparks.

A perfect porcelain face appeared in Belial's vibrant mass. The strain was evident in his voice as he spoke in clipped tones.

"Get out of here! I can't hold him for long!"

Lucifer heard the voice too and realised that he had been tricked. I wondered for a brief moment why Belial would try to save us; maybe he believed our quest had some chance? It wouldn't matter to him if we didn't get out of this. Sometimes you can analyse things too much, though.

Lucifer howled with rage and struggled to free himself from Belial's clutches. I wasn't an expert in angelic combat, but it didn't look like Belial would be able to hold Lucifer for long. The other angels remained weakened from Belial's initial assault, so he pushed more of his form into his grip on Lucifer.

On the far side of the monumental clash, Lazarus watched me while trying to find a way across. I didn't think he'd find a way and, while I would have happily fought him, it would have to wait.

Behind us, where had been glass walls lay open to the sky. I edged to the lip and looked down. It was a long way to the ground.

"How do we get down?" I asked the others.

They all took a look.

"I can get down easily," Hemal told us.

"Well, can you carry us down there?"

"Yes, but only two at a time."

"Well, get started then. Take Hammond and the Friar and then come back for me."

Hemal grasped the Friar and Hammond and vanished. I turned back to the battle and saw that Lucifer had gained the upper hand, forcing Belial backwards. One of the lesser angels had also recovered and joined her master in his assault against Belial.

The battle between the giants no longer filled the room and Lazarus grinned as he saw an opening to reach me. His will snaked through the battle and cold fingers scraped across my head. I shivered at the attack, but the fingers didn't penetrate.

His smile faltered for a second. He recovered quickly and circled the room to get closer. I couldn't unleash my will at him, but I did prepare for a more physical confrontation. Memories of our previous encounters flashed through my mind. I'd beaten him once before in a far from fair fight.

His grin widened as he approached, eyes still sparkling with the view of infinite dimensions. As an immortal human he'd been powerful; now I wondered how much greater he had become.

I took a step towards him and he looked so happy to see me we might have been old friends. Without my abilities I didn't know how events would unfold, but I certainly wouldn't back down.

Annoyance marred his happy expression as firm hands gripped my shoulders and everything disappeared from sight.

Chapter 27
Slice and Dice

Another blink and I lay sprawled on a sea of glass at the foot of the tower. Disorientated for a few seconds by the translocation, I had fallen as we reappeared. Hammond clasped my arm to help me stand, and I nodded my thanks to him.

I looked up the tower which split the sky in two. My view was confused by the interplay of energy high up at the top. Concussive booms shook the ground and rendered conversation impossible.

The Friar waved his hand in front of my face and pointed away from the tower to the city. I agreed — we had to get out of here. We ran away from the tower. Hemal could have escaped easily on her own, but kept with us.

More violent explosions shook the ground and then a gaunt silence fell. I turned around and almost slipped. A bright light, whiter than any explosion, seared my vision. The tower was discernible only as a thin line at the centre of the cloud of light.

The silence deepened as the light increased in brightness until it obscured the sky. Then I heard a chorus of bells, so quiet that at first I didn't recognise them. The light faded and the tower shattered. Giant shards of glass detonated in every direction. I dropped to the floor; the Friar and Hammond followed my lead.

Hemal's first instinct was to protect us. As she leapt between us and the exploding tower, a shard of glass as big as my leg tore through her at ballistic speed. She cried out and I pulled her down as more razor-edged missiles sliced through the air.

The storm last only a few seconds, but might have been hours. The glass screamed as it swept above us. We flattened ourselves as much as possible against the ground, trying to avoid the lethal tempest. When the whistles stopped we all looked at the tower and saw that it had gone.

A sound like cracking ice surrounded us and to our horror cracks appeared in the glass. A quick glance confirmed that the cracks appeared in all directions and all the way to the horizon.

Hemal looked dazed. I gripped her face and forced her to look at me. The hole in her chest gaped open so wide I marvelled at how she remained alive. She grunted, her face drawn in pain.

"We need to get out of here now," I told her.

She nodded, but her eyes remained unfocused.

It was too late by then anyway. The glass around us splintered and collapsed and we dropped into a pit. Debris from the glass plain lined the pit and pierced us as we fell into it. The walls collapsed and widened the pit, accelerating until the plain formed a desert of broken glass.

I thought I'd known agony when the miracle had been torn from my flesh, but that dwindled to a pinprick compared to falling into a sea of broken glass. The glass ground into our bodies and we all cried out, an unsynchronised choir of pain.

The act of twisting to see how the others fared sliced me all over, and I cried out only for razor fragments to fill my mouth. The others shared my agony with their own. Hemal suffered the worst — the thousands of tiny cuts prevented her healing the large tear in her chest. More of the fragments had entered her wound, cutting her deeper from the inside.

The glass crunched like sand as we tried to get up, to reduce the contact points with our bodies, but we collapsed driving fresh shards into ourselves.

"We need to get out of here," I urged the others and crawled away from where the tower once stood. Swimming through broken glass is as painful as it sounds. Back in the real world we wouldn't have survived for long. Death by a thousand cuts would have overwhelmed us and we would have bled out.

Things worked differently here. Our bodies bled and screamed with the pain because that is what bodies do. Our memories of our bodies were too ingrained into our psyches and because of that we suffered. The body-shapes of our souls worked differently, though. They healed quickly and no real blood was lost.

So we experienced pain with each movement. Our bodies were slick with blood, but we kept moving. We dragged the barely-coherent Hemal along as we crawled across the glass.

We continued onwards and then the thing I most feared in that moment happened: the walls of the pit collapsed on top of us. Our torment grew worse than crawling across the razor fragments. We were trapped under an avalanche of agony, swimming through the tiny shards. Our hands, our legs and our faces were all torn. The cuts healed quickly only for fresh wounds to be opened.

The pain became so bad that we had to stop and rest, holding our bodies as still as possible to give them time to heal and the pain to fade. Once restored, if only a little, we swam on. A new fear rose as we moved — how would we know what direction to head in?

We had to reach the tunnels; escape over the surface would be impossible. Lazarus and his allies would surely be looking for us. For all we knew they might be above us now, casually watching and enjoying our torment.

The cycle repeated endlessly, a few minutes of crawling through the glass until the pain became too much. Progress was slow — too slow — and not knowing if we were heading to safety or not weighed upon our minds.

Even though we rested, Hemal didn't seem to recover. The big wound kept tearing open whenever we moved. We contemplated leaving her, allowing her to heal on her own, but the Friar and Hammond both vetoed the idea. Instead we tried resting for longer although it didn't seem to make any difference.

None of us understood why she couldn't heal. Maybe she had too many fragments inside her. The Friar tried his abilities. He gave up after a few minutes, describing it as a black hole which drained the energy without healing the wound. We had little choice but to keep dragging her with us.

We needed a real plan — a way out of this pit, and ultimately a way out of Hell. Beyond that I had no idea. For now just escaping the pain would suffice. The tunnels offered sanctuary, but they lay on the other side of Hell and I didn't know where.

If I hadn't already been in a tremendous amount of pain I would have slapped myself for my stupidity. At the very least I could find the direction we needed to head in. I stopped and told the others my plan.

It proved easy enough to find the direction we needed and to my surprise we were already moving in roughly the right way. I moved through the broken glass without any pain or impediment. I also took the time to search around to see where our pursuers were.

That proved more difficult. I saw trails in the wreckage of the tower, but they vanished. I assumed that the angels had translocated. I probed at the trails hoping to learn more about their source, but they lacked definition despite how recent they appeared.

After learning nothing I swept the area to see if I could discover any other traces. I thought it likely they would have left watchers. Lazarus certainly wanted to spend time with me. Again I discovered nothing and so returned to my body.

The Friar had spent the time considering our next move and filled me in when I opened my eyes. I was also startled to discover that time had passed while I had journeyed. Perhaps this was some sign of my inner reality drawing closer to the one around me.

"I've thought of a way we can reach the tunnels."

"Ok, tell me."

"We make our own tunnel."

It made sense — or at least I understood the potential for it.

"I see. How do we do that?"

"Human souls created the tunnels in the first place. We can do the same."

"I understand, but how?"

"There must be a way. Others have already transformed themselves in this way; I'm sure we can do it too."

I thought about what the Friar had said. It had to be worth a try. Anything would be better than crawling through the endless shards.

"All right, I'll give it a try."

I lay back, covered in the mass of fragments, and focused on my form. I didn't need to leave my body so I felt sure that I could manage this transformation. Pride once again drove me to make the attempt. I wanted to prove that I still had use.

The press of millions of sharp points puncturing my skin made concentration difficult, so I first had to retreat from the pain. I didn't manage that completely, but I pulled back enough to draw my will and push it into the outer shell of my form.

With my will in my current human shape I moulded a new form, a cylindrical shape, and the smallest of tunnels — after all, you have to start somewhere. My form resisted. It remembered what shape it wanted to be and didn't like my instructions to change. I poured my will into pushing the change, hoping it would be like shaping clay. In reality it behaved more like the clay had been fired.

That realisation gave me pause; perhaps I approached this problem from the wrong direction. Before making my body change I had to make it malleable or I risked causing damage. Worse, the damage might not be repairable.

My body had only ever known one shape, but that shape had changed in small ways over the years, so it wasn't completely unused to change. I used my will to tease the changes it had known; small mutations, nothing too dramatic to start with.

I stretched at the skin, pushed at it, moved it in all directions. Inch by inch I urged small changes and gradually my body eased its rigid resistance. As I mastered control of my shape I moved away from the small variations and pushed for more dramatic changes.

With the greater changes the glass once again sliced into my flesh, disturbing my concentration and halting my progress. More foolishness on my part. If I changed the form of my body then couldn't I also modify the structure of it too? The tunnels we had travelled through weren't made of flesh, after all.

I should have tried that in the first place. Skin isn't the best of building materials and so I experienced problems trying to turn myself into a tunnel. I transformed my body into a sheathe of fluidic plastic and then I enclosed my friends, so they were protected from the glass.

For now at any rate.

Chapter 28
One after the Other

I'd mastered the art of becoming a tunnel, and believe me, that felt like quite an accomplishment. The first benefit was no more pain — at least, not from the smashed glass. I revelled in that absence for a while and then extended myself in the direction we needed to go. I didn't take long to discover the limit to how far I could reach. Inside me the others walked from one end to the other.

When they reached the far end the Friar communicated with me and I shared the knowledge of how I became a tunnel — not the most significant of secrets I'll admit, but damn useful in the circumstances.

With my guidance, the Friar mastered the technique quickly. He wrapped one end of his tunnel around me. I then restored my usual human form and helped Hammond move Hemal to the far end.

Hemal looked in bad shape. Her wound still hadn't healed and I worried at what might have made her unable to restore herself. From what I understood she should have healed a wound like this over time. She had no anatomy, so no organs to damage other than the hole in her chest.

I examined her wound, hoping to find some clue, or anything that might have caused her healing to fail. The edges of the wound were ragged. As expected I saw no bleeding, but nor did I see the complexity of form I'd seen inside her before. I detected hints of it — eddies in the currents of her being.

Inside, the wound felt cold to the touch and the barely-visible eddies responded to my probing. It seemed reasonable to guess that was the cause of her inability to heal, although why it had occurred I didn't know.

The Friar completed his section and then Hammond took his turn. Leapfrogging each other gave us time to regain a fraction of our energy, but the transformation back and forth sapped our strength and it took more time each cycle to fully recover.

It didn't matter; we now made good progress. It might not have been as quick as travelling on the surface or following the already constructed tunnels, but we headed in the direction we needed to go — more or less. At least we moved away from the wreckage of Belial's tower unhindered.

To add to the general feeling of positivity Hemal showed some small signs of improvement. She even regained consciousness after several dozen cycles. The wound still gaped open like a hungry mouth and it worried me that I still didn't see any signs of the complexity within her essence around the wound.

When she finally remained lucid enough for conversation, I asked her why her wound wasn't healing.

"I'm not sure," she answered.

Not the answer I wanted.

"I inspected the wound and it looks like it's changed your insides in some way."

"I was struck by a fragment from the domain of a powerful angel. Domains are built from the essence of their creators. For angels that can be separate from their personal forms, although their domains are still part of them."

"I don't understand."

"It would be like Belial punching me clear through my body. With his power the shock would impact my structure on every level."

"I still don't get it."

"You've seen my inner essence, glimpsed our true form?"

I remembered the overwhelming complexity of Lucifer and his minions facing off against Belial.

"The richness of form grows with us; when we are injured it simplifies. This makes it easier to heal. The complexity returns as it regenerates."

I guessed it made some sort of sense. That explanation would have to do, as my turn to create the next tunnel had come. After a few more cycles, while the Friar moved us forward I enquired about how we would reach Heaven.

"It won't be easy." Her voice sounded weak, but clear.

"Why not?"

"We have to reach Heaven. That won't be as easy as it was to get into Hell."

"Why not?"

"The tunnels don't go to Heaven, not as far as I know anyway. Michael is a lot stricter about contact with unaffiliated humans than Lucifer. He considers your kind a corrupting influence and his forces will also ensure compliance."

"How far will the tunnels get us?"

"To the border if we're lucky, but I don't know what the situation is up there at the moment. When I last visited there all out war raged along the border between Heaven and Eden."

"Can we go around the fighting? Sneak in around the flanks?" Hammond asked.

"Maybe, but it would be a long journey. Who knows what the situation will be by then?"

"Hemal's right," I said. "The confusion is our only advantage; we need to use it. If we get there after Lucifer has won the battle we don't know if Metatron will even still be alive."

"Is Michael still using human forces in his armies?" Hammond enquired.

"Yes, they believe there is a place in Heaven for them."

I saw where Hammond was going with that. "How are they identified?"

"They have to be under the command of a loyalist angel."

"So there's our way in."

"It won't be easy. I would imagine that the border is utter chaos with constant conflict and moving away from the front lines will be tricky."

"Understood, but it gives us a plan and we can assess the situation when we get there. First we have to reach the old tunnel network and return to Eden."

With a vague plan in mind we pushed towards Eden one section at a time until we connected with the existing tunnels. We rested for a short while I scouted the path we needed to follow.

We had entered a different part of the network to the one we'd used while travelling to Hell. It looked the same, but when I delved into myself to look around I found trails everywhere. These tunnels appeared to be much more heavily-travelled than the ones we'd used before and inspired a sense of foreboding. We'd avoided contact with the creatures that inhabited these tunnels so far, but on those occasions they had been lone hunters; here I suspected a larger group operated.

Perhaps Hammond would get his wish and we'd have to be more aggressive against these shriekers. In truth I wouldn't have minded a confrontation. There had been too much running away for my liking recently and sometimes you need to smash a few skulls (even if only figuratively) to release that pent up feeling.

We were all still exhausted from building our pathway. With hindsight it might have been prudent to rest more than we did, but we still had a long way to go and not much time to do so.

So we cautiously followed my lead and it came as no surprise when the first shrieks echoed towards us from the remote darkness in the tunnels.

Chapter 29
Angel Delight

This time we heard more than a single shriek. I counted four, maybe five different voices as we moved through the tunnels. For a while they kept their distance, but it also meant that we daren't stop.

After a few hours we took a chance and stopped, just long enough for me to delve into myself and make sure that we still headed in the right direction. I also took the opportunity to scout for the shriekers. I found their trails, but not a live sighting.

As before, the tunnels twisted in a maze. With my inner vision I kept us heading the right way, but soon the shrieks came from both ahead and behind.

Still I didn't catch any glimpse of them.

They made their move while we rested. I was deep inside my mental model of the world and didn't hear them. Dozens of them screeched as they charged up the tunnel towards us. They attacked from both directions and swarmed over us.

I saw their trails but not in the instances of my memory. The attack revealed a flaw in my construct. It contained the past, to an extent, but not the present.

The mental map hadn't let me down, but probably because it was permanent, immutable. I recalled previous instances; I'd seen my friends, but they were from existing memories.

My mind drifted with the puzzle while the Friar and Hammond desperately battled the mob of shrieking creatures, eager to consume our souls.

When I finally finished chasing the conundrum it was too late. We'd been overwhelmed, and the shriekers dragged us down the tunnel. They looked like ghouls from an old horror movie, their skin sallow and grey, smeared with crusted remains from their previous meals.

They no longer shrieked their hungry howl; instead they sang with jubilation. Three of them carried me in a bouncing lope. Despite their thin bodies they moved at a fast pace with an easy, loping stride. I struggled, seeking to escape and the lead one stumbled.

The small opportunity disappeared as two more rushed in and grabbed my arms. I struggled again. This time they maintained their grip and we continued our bumpy journey down the tunnel.

I searched around as best I could, trying to locate the others. Three of the revenants held the Friar secure just ahead of me. As I expected, Hammond caused them more trouble and he still roared with fury as a small mob of them dragged him along.

Hemal must have been somewhere behind me. I couldn't see her directly although I did see a larger mob who sang with greater glee. I guessed with the four of us they had caught themselves quite the feast.

Their faces gleamed with horrible lust, their desire for our flesh drooling from their mouths. I didn't enjoy the sight, so I distracted myself by wondering where they would take us.

We discovered our destination all too soon when a blast of fire scorched me and surrounded us. The stench of charred flesh smelled sweet in my mouth. Thousands of voices cried out in welcome — horrible hungry sounds.

I wished we were back in the tunnels.

The shriekers' domain was a realm of torment. Cliffs surrounded us, and yellow steam belched out of pores on the rock. Creatures that had once been human stood naked in front of larger holes, almost sexless, their skin grey and tight.

They sang a terrible song like a murder of crows celebrating a roadkill feast. They jumped up and down in excitement, hooting as if they had devolved into beasts of the jungle.

The domain appeared small. In a glance I beheld its range, no more than a village carved into the encircling cliffs. The press of our captors prevented me from seeing our destination, but once again we didn't have to wait long.

A brief pain blossomed as they threw me to the ground, which was rocky covered in loose dirt. These creatures — these people — had built themselves a primitive Hell. Our captors held us, but allowed us to sit and see what waited before us.

A crude altar stood before us, carved from the same brown veined rock which towered above us on all sides. A single shrieker stood by this altar. Unlike the others who all appeared of indeterminate age this one looked ancient beyond years.

Where the others lacked hair, his hung in matted ropes all the way to his waist. Unlike the rest of his tribe who lacked clothing, he wore filthy skins that I guessed came from captives like us who'd been caught in their snare. He held his thin arms into the sky and a hush fell across the assembled shriekers. They stopped their prancing and watched their leader intently.

Hammond cursed loudly and the guards silenced him with a flurry of savage blows. The old man ignored the interruption and spoke to his tribe. To my surprise I discovered that I understood every word.

"My children, our hunters have returned with a feast which will sustain us in this dark time. The chaos of nullity blesses our hunters' effort for they have brought one of the blessed ones for our nourishment."

A moan of awed desire washed through the gathering. The old man motioned them to be silent.

"We should rejoice for this gift, this treasure, this bounty which will be our feast."

The throng moaned again, although it sounded more like a prayer this time. The old man nodded in satisfaction.

"Not only are we grateful for this most precious treasure, we are also thrice more blessed — not by the divine, but by those touched by the divine. They will be our storehouse for the hard times to come."

Again the crowd moaned, this time in thanks for their bounty. I wondered if the old man knew of what had happened to the Earth. With no fresh souls what would these creatures feed on?

In truth I didn't care, but my mind enjoyed following random puzzles. It also distracted me from what loomed in our future.

I wished it had, but it didn't — at least not for long.

"And now we shall taste of the blessed one's flesh, a feast which we haven't enjoyed for centuries. Bring it to the altar!"

At his command the shriekers holding Hemal dragged her towards the altar. She resisted, but she lacked any real strength and with contemptuous ease they manhandled her onto the altar where she lay spread-eagled. Several of them gripped her pale arms and legs while the old man shuffled beside her and bent to one of hands.

He then bit into her flesh.

The others took that as their signal to join the feast. Each took a bite before another took their place and tore another chunk of flesh from the prostrate angel. Her skin was obviously tougher than they expected; most of them required several attempts to tear their bite free.

One by one the shriekers took their place next to Hemal and bit and chewed and as they left the expression on their faces looked the same. The taste for them was clearly sublime — beggars used to scraps now eating the finest cuisine.

Hemal screamed.

The sound of her screams eclipsed the sickening bites and chewing sounds of her flesh being removed.

I lunged from my guards' grip. The Friar and Hammond did the same. We surprised our captors who had been engrossed by the sight of their feasting friends. Despite the advantage of surprise we didn't even get close.

We fought, of course; how could we not? Hemal's screams rose in volume and pitch with each bite. Already dozens of the filthy beasts had taken their portions. Hundreds more lined up to do the same.

The guards swarmed us. They battered us in a haphazard fashion; they wanted to join the feast and so beat us with just enough weight to halt our efforts. Subdued, they forced us to watch as more and more quivering chunks were torn from Hemal's body.

The ritual of Hemal's consumption lasted for hours. Each took their turn and left to chew the angel flesh in contentment. Her screams turned into howls and she continued screaming until only small remnants of her once beautiful face remained.

The leader placed the final remnant of Hemal into his mouth and chewed with evident satisfaction.

By this point all had eaten their ration and the domain filled with the sound of chewing. Angel meat obviously didn't go down easily. Thankfully the screaming had stopped. Beside me the Friar openly wept. Hammond remained silent and his face was rigid with anger.

Chapter 30
Up Next

I stared at the altar, which was empty now and had been for some time. Raiding parties of shriekers left the domain every so often, although we remained surrounded by guards. We tried to escape, but with the same predictable result. Their numbers held us secure.

The raiding parties always returned empty-handed and when they did so the old man glanced at us. We understood what that meant, of course, but they wouldn't allow us to talk. Whenever we tried our guards beat us until we understood the message.

Meaningful glances became our only means of communication.

So we waited. Our fate appeared certain; the only unknown was when. They didn't allow me to delve inside myself. I didn't understand how our guards knew, but whenever I tried they hurt me to bring me back. The pain didn't always work; I'd developed a reasonable tolerance over the years. The old man had a trick, though. He would spit on my face which always brought me back, although I could not understand why that worked.

The wait dragged indeterminably with no way to pass the time: a mundane horror of seconds taking their time to pass from one to the next. It afforded time for thinking, but only surface thoughts were permitted. Deep contemplation was treated harshly; our captors assumed this to be the same as delving, and maybe they were right.

I'd accumulated a number of puzzles in the time since my transformation, the most pressing of which remained my inability to project my will beyond the physical limits of my body. Sure, I'd found a workaround for that limitation, but I needed my abilities back. I considered myself a lesser being because of that weakness.

Escape was the other driving imperative occupying my attention. Hundreds of these shriekers populated the domain. I wondered if they inhabited only this domain, or if other tribes existed. I had no real way of knowing, but in the scheme of things I didn't think it really mattered.

One on one we could handle them; we'd even be able to overpower a small group. I watched them to learn their behaviour. The old man squatted by the altar. He usually remained silent, and I suspected he entered a trance state. I wondered what strange dimensions he explored.

Not for the first time, I became frustrated by the way my mind now seemed happy to wander even in these urgent circumstances.

The rest of the tribe rested in their hovels: what appeared to be small caves cut into the rocks. They only moved when a raiding party left, encouraging them with a song of hope.

They would gather again when the hunters returned, always with a song of lamentation when they saw that they'd returned without victims.

How many times did I watch them return?

It reached a point when I found myself hoping they'd find someone, because I knew that eventually they would pick one of us to fill their hungry bellies. Whenever they came empty-handed the entire tribe would stare at us and then at the old man beseechingly. He always shook his head and they would slump, hunger drawn on their faces.

How long would his will hold them until their hunger overrode his authority?

Eventually the dreaded time came. Instead of shaking his head he pointed at me, and my guards pulled me towards the altar. I fought them every inch of the way with all my fury. I heard the Friar and Hammond bellowing with rage as they tried to help. All of our efforts proved useless, but that didn't stop us from trying. Hammond and the Friar battled until their guards beat them unconscious.

In my case they didn't mind me resisting. Maybe it made the meat taste better. They didn't subdue me with blows. Instead more of them gripped my limbs and forced me to the altar.

I fought even while bent over the altar, although by then there were so many shriekers on each of my limbs I barely moved.

The old man spoke no words this time. Instead he sang in joy — a harsh vocalisation of thanks and the entire tribe responded in kind. The press of dirty bodies against me muffled their cries. Warm saliva drooled onto my skin.

I tensed my muscles, anticipating what was about to happen. If I tensed my muscles enough they wouldn't be able to take a bite. The old man went first and to my surprise it didn't hurt too much.

When he tore the chunk free from my side, the initial shock blazed in an agony which shattered that delusion. I screamed worthy of a low budget horror film and the sound provided the trigger for the others holding me to join the feast. They didn't rush. Each took their time and savoured the taste as they bit into my flesh. I heard nothing but the satisfied moans and closing of jaws.

And my screams, of course.

I howled like a trapped beast. Each bite forced a fresh scream. My cries carried a terrible harmony to the chomping of teeth and the eager breathing of the hungry.

Eager hands held me firm and smothered my frantic struggles. No matter how hard I fought I couldn't move by even the smallest amount. I raged with pain and anger, my voice the only pitiful release I had against this torment.

The pain became my only constant. So many mouths tore at my flesh I received no pause in this slow consumption of my body. I realised that I couldn't fight my way free, but perhaps there was another way I could escape.

I'd known great pain before. The agony of the miracle's fire which once consumed my flesh without mercy was much like the teeth of these degenerates chewing upon me now. Then I had escaped by withdrawing into myself, taking sanctuary in the infinite depths of my mind.

I withdrew inwards, following the recursive patterns of my form, a fractal pattern shared with all of creation around me. As I descended into my body the bites followed me; with each bite I grew weaker, my essence torn from my being. It made concentration difficult. I wanted to get as far away from the pain as possible, but each bite drew me back.

Time slipped like a heartbeat as I froze the memory of the moment from which I'd just passed. Locked in the frozen moment, I no longer experienced the pain and that felt like ultimate bliss. I existed in that absence of pain for as long as I could.

Naturally, reality continued its course. I hadn't frozen the passage of time, only my perception of it for a single instant. It worked as a temporary escape, but didn't provide a real reprieve. Moment by moment more bites of my essence were ripped from my body and I weakened further.

I needed a better plan. Being absent from the pain provided an opportunity for contemplation; I'd bought myself time, but delving deeper into myself would only delay the inevitable. Escape would have to follow a different route.

There was no escape inward and I couldn't fight my way free. What other options did I have?

Reality.

The essence of reality formed the same structures in me as it did in the surrounding domain. In the same way, when we transformed into the tunnels we remained ourselves.

There was the answer.

I smiled as a hungry shrieker chewed off my lips and I filtered myself into the altar.

Howls of fury echoed around the domain as my tasty essence vanished from their grasp. They clawed at the stone of the altar, shouting and seeking to drag me from it. I watched them paw and grasp, amused by their futile efforts. The pain from my body faded as I pushed my will into the ragged wounds and restored my form.

My confidence slipped as the old man pushed his flock away and touched the stone. I sensed his will flex against the altar, probing at its structure as he searched for me. His will tasted bitter as it touched mine and I pushed back. We clashed, straining against each other like wrestlers until I collapsed deeper into the rock. I tricked him into overextending himself and with the same motion I tore a chunk of his essence and subsumed it into my own will.

And it tasted divine.

In a strange paradox it also contained a foul undertone, but the energy I received from the morsel overcame the odd taste and restored the strength I'd lost. The old man possessed great strength. The taste of him might have been terrible, but it certainly hit the spot.

He didn't enjoy the reversal of roles and withdrew from the stone. He gibbered and gestured towards the Friar and Hammond. The mob surged at them. I didn't know if they'd seen my vanishing trick.

When they saw the empty altar they must have assumed that I had been completely devoured. Grief and anger filled their voices as they raged against their captors. Their efforts availed them as little as mine had me.

The altar shifted and expanded around me. I responded by expanding myself as well; all the better to detect another attack from the old man. I sensed the old man focus his will and guessed that he was preparing something to prevent the Friar and Hammond from pulling the same trick I had.

The mob dragged them to the altar and stretched them across the stone. They kept fighting as I had done and screamed as the teeth tore into their bodies.

Aware that I couldn't help them, I hid safe inside the stone. It seemed a reasonable assumption that only the old man could use his will against me in the fabric of the domain. On the other hand I didn't want to watch Hammond and the Friar being eaten alive, so I pushed out of the stone and attacked the shriekers.

My reappearance surprised the ones near to me and I launched a violent albeit short-lived counter attack. The Friar and Hammond continued to scream; they were so lost in their agony they didn't even comprehend I had returned.

All too quickly, my screams joined theirs and I tried to retreat into the stone. This time the old man was prepared. He probably hadn't believed his luck when I emerged from the stone, but he certainly wouldn't let me use the same means to escape again.

Chapter 31
Unexpected Saviour

I returned to the endless ocean of pain. At least this time I didn't drown alone; not that this made any real difference on a practical level, but I took some comfort in knowing that someone else endured the same experience as me.

I realise how that sounds.

The mind wanders and sometimes it takes you along unexpected paths. This time some of my old self returned. I didn't try to escape it; instead I revelled in my exquisite suffering. Pride might have been my major failing, but it also provided my strength.

Odd to think of pride in a situation like this. The pain boiled and exploded around my being, but it didn't hurt. I didn't notice at first, but when I did it returned with a vengeance. I howled, no longer a solo, but in a trio with the Friar and Hammond.

Hammond naturally provided the bass.

With that whimsical thought the pain submerged again. This time I flowed with the sensation rather than allow myself to be surprised by it. I examined the odd feeling. My body rippled and I understood why the pain had gone away.

Without conscious direction, my mind had determined a way to save myself from being eaten alive (so to speak). How it had done so remained a mystery. My best guess was that the flights of fancy my mind had been taking allowed another part of me to process. I didn't know what that part might be, and to be honest I didn't really care.

My body saved itself from being devoured. As a shrieker took a bite the skin shrank away so the bite contained no flesh, or a scrape at most. Instead of the constant agony it tickled. I became overwhelmed by the oddness of it and laughed.

I laughed out loud — a ridiculous response, especially as next to me Hammond and the Friar were still being eaten by the mob. My body's weird defence saved me, but didn't free me from the shriekers who held us down against the altar.

Surrounded by their screams and the grunts of those feeding, I tried again to free myself from their clutches. Their numbers held me down. I launched my will at them, intending to spear them with it. My flesh had become more malleable and the lances of my will forced my form into an outward burst of spikes.

The sudden transformation hurt, but not as much as being eaten. I doubted anything could be, although pain provided the realisation that I'd been successful. As I'd launched the attack I remembered my inability to unleash my will beyond the confines of my body.

An instant later, thanks to my body having learnt that it was subject to my will, I resembled a hedgehog on steroids. Poles of my flesh impaled the shriekers that held me to the altar. It didn't kill them, but it did give them something new to focus on. I restored my form and pushed up from the altar.

They had never seen such a thing before and even the old man appeared surprised as I rose off the stone. I didn't care; my first efforts were to free the Friar and Hammond. I attacked the shriekers who fed on them. They were too busy to sense my approach.

I attacked with brutal detachment, smashing and tearing at their bodies until I'd cleared some space around the altar. So focused was I on the attack I didn't even take the time to enjoy it. The Friar and Hammond looked in bad shape. Large holes ruined their bodies. For several seconds they didn't realise that they had been freed and continued to scream and convulse.

When they did realise, they opened and their eyes and saw me looming over them.

"Heal yourselves," I instructed. "We don't have much time."

In fact we had no time at all; the surrounding tribe surged at us. I fought desperately, trying to buy enough time for Hammond and the Friar to join the fight.

The Friar recovered first. He saw the method I had used to engage the mass of attacking shriekers and immediately followed the same pattern. Spears of his being lanced out and struck through the bodies of the attackers. They cried out as the lances punched through them, but they weren't out of the fight.

When he had restored himself, Hammond used a different method to join the fray. He bludgeoned those who came too close. All the while the old man danced and shrieked a warbling song to encourage his followers.

And they kept coming.

Individually we were stronger, despite our recent injuries, but the shriekers didn't stay down easily. The altar provided us with a small advantage which we used to good effect. They had the numbers, but only a few could effectively attack us at once.

We started off stronger, but the intense fight drained our strength. We'd grown accustomed to transforming our shapes, but it still took focus to do so and they provided no respite — they just kept coming.

We lost track of time in the battle; we fought and the Friar fell first. Two of the shriekers lunged at him. He speared one through the face, but only grazed the other and the shrieker capitalised on the Friar's mistake. She grabbed his legs and pulled him off balance.

The Friar reacted quickly and his legs extruded into a cloud of spears which almost disintegrated the shrieker. Her companions filled the gap and he didn't have the time to recover his footing. He fought and they kept pushing until they isolated him from Hammond and myself.

We saw him fall and tried to help. The press of attackers prevented us from doing more than maintaining our own fight. I saw him go under a pile of bodies. He screamed again as they bit into his flesh.

With only the two of us defending the altar, not long passed before another of us fell; this time it was me. Hammond tried to rescue me and immediately found himself overwhelmed. They wrenched me from the altar and I could no longer see what was happening.

I cried out as teeth sank into my flesh once again. I blasted a swarm of spears into the mob crushing me. I lacked the force to stop them all and their frenzied bites sapped my strength all the more.

It looked like the end, but help came from the most unexpected source.

At first we didn't recognise that we were being rescued. We had our own troubles holding our attention. The first inkling came in the howls of many shriekers as they were shredded. I didn't know they were being shredded at that point, of course; first came the sound and only afterwards did understanding arrive.

They separated us after overwhelming us, dragging us across the ground so that we couldn't unite. They fed on us. With the new noise I increased my efforts, fearing what it heralded. I dredged more strength from my ever-diminishing reserves. I'd like to claim that I freed myself, but that was far from the case.

A dervish of energies ripped through the mob holding me. They disintegrated into vapour. I had enough strength left to take advantage of the opening and absorbed the spray of shriekers into my being.

The rush held me for a second as the remnants infused me. I blinked and beheld death annihilate the tribe. I'd seen these forces before, in Belial's tower. How I recognised them presented a new puzzle; somehow I recognised the interplay of geometric form and energy as a unique signature.

They were awesome to behold and they made no pretence of appearing human. Here stood angels in their true form. They shifted form and colour seemingly at random as they unleashed immense fury on the tribe.

The shriekers didn't take the assault without resistance. They mobbed the two angels as they had done to us. They might as well have thrown themselves into a threshing machine. One particularly bold group managed to swarm one of the angels, only to be reduced to chaff and consumed by the towering force.

I could now stand and looked for Hammond and the Friar. The Friar was now free and faced one of the angels. The other angel carved a path towards Hammond. I then spotted Lazarus up on the cliffs gorging upon the remains of several shriekers.

The sight of him froze me for a moment. Until that point I hadn't considered why the angels had attacked the shriekers. I hoped, of course — as anyone would — that someone had come to rescue us. Seeing Lazarus added a dark complication to that thought.

The Friar stood and looked at the approaching angel in confusion. The angel enveloped him with its essence and then moved away. I shouted for them to stop and rushed to follow. The shriekers hadn't forgotten me despite their heavy losses and several of them tackled me.

I fought them off while the other angel slaughtered the shriekers attacking Hammond — before snatching him away as well. The Friar and Hammond had both been taken.

After killing the last shrieker I looked up at Lazarus; his face was fat with a happy grin. He turned and followed the cliff towards the boundary of the domain and vanished from sight. I then realised that the two angels were no longer visible either.

This left me alone facing the survivors of the decimated tribe.

And they looked pissed.

Chapter 32
No Choice at All

The shriekers faced me over the scant remains of their brethren. There didn't appear to be many of them left — perhaps less than a quarter of their original number, although enough remained to pose a threat as I faced them alone. I didn't blame them for being pissed; I would have been too in their shoes. I had to follow Lazarus as quickly as possible. I didn't know what he wanted with Hammond and the Friar, but I was willing to bet that it wouldn't be pleasant for either of them.

I first considered blending into the fabric of the domain again and sneaking out. The old man must have had the same thought; he blocked that option with his will. I would have to fight my way through.

The decision made, I surged forward and extended my body into a line of spears which stabbed through the nearest of them. Taking the offensive surprised them and it provided me with a small advantage. My initial attack knocked several of them down. After a moment of indecision they surged forward.

By that point I was already moving. Not towards the group; instead I charged at the old man. His followers were caught off guard by the move, but the old man appeared less surprised and he ran towards the safety of the crowd.

I cast more spears of my body towards the group, hoping to distract them long enough for me to reach the old man. I saw him reach his tribe and in desperation I lashed myself out like a whip, coiled my essence around his legs and knocked him to the ground.

Again the mob was stunned by my move and that bought me a few more seconds. I smothered him completely with my body, his muffled cries warm and damp against my skin. I squeezed with all my strength and crushed the old man. He fought for freedom, clawed at my skin, all to no avail. His cries became screeches as I heard a pop and crushed the old man's wiry frame.

I squeezed until his movements ceased and then absorbed the mangled remains. The rush I'd experienced after consuming his minions was nothing compared to this. The old man had been ancient, possibly the oldest of his kind. I suspected that he had been one of the earliest humans to have succumbed to the desire to subsist on his fellow men.

He had feasted on thousands of humans over the millennia. He had helped build the tunnels and stalked the human souls who took refuge in them from the angelic raiding parties.

His spirit tasted divine and richly flavoured with his knowledge and experience. The depth of his flavour was spiced with his malevolence and subtly layered by those he had fed on. I revelled in it, the surge of it beyond any drug I might have imagined. If I had known about this during my experimentation days then the path of my life might have been very different. Probably not for the better.

Enraged yells interrupted the sublime reverie and dragged me back into the filth of the domain. The old man's barrier no longer existed, so I had the power to simply escape at that point — if I chose to do so.

I didn't leave.

I slaughtered them all. Like a junkie after his first hit I wanted more. These morsels didn't come close to the old man's juicy spirit, but I enjoyed them all the same. It didn't take long to kill each and every one of them. I didn't take my time, but I didn't rush either. The imperative to follow Hammond and the Friar had been drowned out by the high I now chased.

Like all good things, the high faded and I stood alone in the empty domain. The afterglow of the sensation took a little longer to fade and it wasn't until it did that I thought once again of Hammond and the Friar.

The domain crumbled with the death of the tribe. Its reality collapsed. I surged before it vanished completely and gained entrance to the tunnels.

I wasted no further time and delved into myself, seeking the trails of Lazarus and the two angels. It didn't take long to find their path, but they had moved quickly and I had spent too long feasting upon the shriekers so I had much ground to catch up.

The strength of those I had consumed allowed me to move swiftly, but so had those I chased. It didn't really matter that I didn't know their destination. Wherever they went I would follow.

I chased them a great distance, all the way under Hell and into the Garden of Eden. They managed to keep ahead of me no matter how hard I pushed. I saw no sign of Hammond or the Friar in the trails and I hoped that no harm had come to them.

My time on the hunt became one of solitude and I didn't mind that. It allowed my mind to wander. Following the trail took barely any focus, so I toyed with the puzzles of my new existence. I gleaned no real insight, but it did occupy my mind for the time.

I also thought of Lazarus. I'd last been told about his dismemberment and burial across Eden. Had he escaped somehow? Or had he even been condemned in that way at all? Considering events since then, it most likely had been a lie all along. What I did know for certain was that he bore a grudge against me, and for fair reason. I too had an argument with him. He'd caused the first real fear I'd ever felt.

That fear still lingered. I had beaten him before and I yearned to do so again. The strength of those I had consumed still flowed within me, filling me with confidence — arrogance, maybe — but where pride leads arrogance will often follow.

I wanted to kill that fear once and for all.

With those thoughts burning foremost in my mind I followed the trail to its conclusion. After being in the tunnels and the shrieker's domain for so long it felt strange to be on the surface again. The sky looked so huge, the horizon so distant it dwarfed me with its immensity.

Back when blood pumped in my veins I loved to stand and stare up at the night sky, the perfect black studded with stars around which I imagined alien worlds. It's odd — I never considered myself as part of the human machine, always preferring to keep myself separate. Even though it had the power to render me insignificant, the cosmos proved a different matter. I thought, no I knew, that I existed within it.

Now don't get me wrong — I don't mean in the sense that I represented part of God's plan, or even that I owned some special destiny (that came later from other people's mouths). No, the feeling I had was more one of belonging and wonder.

That was a feeling I would never know again, unless I convinced God to make everything right. The task sounded ridiculous when stated plainly like that. The fresh fear of repeated failure twisted with the older terror. I lacked time to entertain doubts, but they surfaced anyway.

Who was to determine what God should do to make the world right? And to convince God what needed to be done? I had never believed in him, so why would he listen to me?

Those doubts assailed my confidence, as did the sight Eden presented. In a vision I'd seen Eden in its original glory, a lush paradise created to welcome human souls after their transformation from life. With my own eyes I had seen it become a battlefield, the beautiful garden churned into a wasteland of mud, thick with the blood of lost souls.

Even in this state it retained some pretence of welcome, even if it was a harsh welcome. Now the death of the world had spilled its molten guts across the garden. The lava had cooled and now an alien landscape filled my vision.

Rock formed gullies and dunes, a frozen grey desert stretching beyond the horizon. A stray thought wondered how far the horizon would be in a world of infinite dimensions. The air hung heavy with the rancid stench of sulphurous gases. The Garden now resembled the fevered imaginings of Hell rather than a place of tranquillity.

The rock still felt warm beneath my feet, mostly firm, and only the occasional footstep sank into the crust. I no longer had to delve into my memory of the world to see the trail. Their impressions sunk into the soft rock were easy for me to follow.

I was grateful that I didn't have far to walk. The fumes made my head swim and my attention wander, although that had happened a lot to me recently anyway.

The group waited for me, although I heard them before I saw them. Even at this distance I could separate their voices — Hammond's hoarse and deep bass, the Friar's lighter, both saturated with pain. I quickened my pace upon hearing their cries and ran with all my will, my legs stretching as if elastic, lengthening my pace and so I covered the ground more quickly.

As I ran, the detached part of me considered what terrible torture caused such screams. I let it wander as a parallel process while my main focus, the new part of me, pushed aside the doubts and fear and unneeded complications and focused only on moving towards the sound.

To most people a scream is just a scream, but that part of me heard something more intricate. There were layers of anguish in those cries, melodies of pain that sang of a master at work.

When they came into view I kept running, taking in the scene with a speeding glance. The Friar and Hammond were fused in two pillars formed from the same rock my feet pounded against. Lazarus stood between them. He swallowed something with evident relish. To one side but nearer to my approach were the geometric clouds of the fallen angels. They didn't have faces or any recognisable features. Despite that, I knew I had their full attention.

They didn't react as I charged towards them. Lazarus stepped up to Hammond and pulled a strip of flesh from the length of his torso. Hammond roared, cursing Lazarus as the ex-disciple rolled the strip and popped it into his mouth.

My detached thoughts ceased pondering the mysteries of screams and noted the sight of the flesh where the skin had been peeled. Hammond's strength had allowed him to heal quickly, ready for Lazarus to peel another morsel, but it would be the Friar's turn next. Before his skin sealed I caught a glimpse of his essence below.

Of course we no longer possessed real bodies, so I wasn't expecting to see exposed muscle (or maybe I did? The bondage of a lifetime of flesh proved hard to shake) and in that respect I wasn't surprised. Instead I witnessed the complex interplay of shapes and geometries I'd seen in Hemal — indeed what I saw in its raw form in the two fallen awaiting my charge.

Why hadn't I noticed that before? It made absolute sense. We were all agents of creation, and the realisation contained a secret that I needed to unravel — but then there was no time because I'd reached the two fallen. Even in my fury I knew that to take them on directly would be a mistake, so instead I tried to slip between them. My plan was simple: free Hammond and the Friar before engaging Lazarus directly.

Not the greatest of plans I'll admit, but sometimes men just can't help acting on impulse.

The Friar looked up and his face twisted in a mask of suffering. He recognised me and cried out a warning, but I didn't even make it past the fallen. They morphed and snared me.

Lazarus turned and smiled a wide, welcoming grin.

"It's been too long, and we have much to discuss."

Chapter 33
Hunting the Saviour

I struggled, I raged, and without effort the fallen held me secure while Lazarus waited patiently for my impotent anger to run its course. I'll admit that it took a while.

"Are you done?" he asked me.

"Don't speak to him; save yourself and forget us," the Friar shouted.

Lazarus snapped the Friar's jaw downward. I heard a crack of bone even though he had no skeleton. With a swift motion Lazarus tore the Friar's tongue from his mouth. No blood poured, only a pitiful cry.

Hammond raged and Lazarus tore his tongue out as well. He swallowed them both, his throat expanding like a snake's to push the meat down his gullet.

"Now we can talk without interruption."

I lost it again, but quickly calmed when his fingers grabbed my own tongue.

"I'm happy to conduct the conversation on my own if you'd prefer."

He pulled on my tongue and I gagged. It hurt — by Christ it hurt — but I refused to give him the satisfaction. I would not submit. He pulled it harder and the root stretched, filling my mouth with fresh agony. He smiled as he watched my struggle to defy him.

"It's just like old times, isn't it?" he taunted. "Now are you going to behave in a civilised fashion?"

I withstood the pain for another minute while he gradually pulled harder. The detached part of me didn't experience the pain. It did advise me to stop being an idiot; why suffer when I didn't need to? I gained nothing from my pride.

The cold part spoke the truth, but it still hurt to nod my surrender.

Not as much as having my tongue ripped out though.

"Good. As I said we have much to discuss and it's much harder for you to talk if you don't have a tongue. Not impossible though."

I'm not sure I wanted to understand what his final comment meant.

"It appears that we share the same goal, you and I."

I kept silent. I understood what he meant, but maybe I would learn something new if I played dumb for a while.

Lazarus nodded his understanding. "Heaven and revenge had been my focus for so long I found it liberating to discover something better. Hell provided me with a greater paradise than the one I'd witnessed with my first death and, even better, they understood my desire.

"This is where you come in. I played a small part in making sure you fulfilled your role in Lucifer's plan. He rewarded me with the knowledge of Jesus; that the so-called Son of God is the last true demon."

His suggestion made sense and, if I had thought about it more, I might have reached the same conclusion. He appeared from nowhere; he wasn't human or an angel. From what I'd been told that left only one possibility. It also explained why he hadn't been seen since his passing.

"I understand you are searching for him as well. You hope that by connecting with his son you will find some way to connect with God and that he will restore the world you knew. Do I speak the truth?"

He did, but I had no intention of telling him that.

"The question was rhetorical anyway. My sources are very reliable."

His glance included the two fallen beside me. They hadn't contributed to the conversation at all. Did they consider interacting with humans beneath them? I decided that I should join the discussion, to see if I could learn anything else of use.

"What do your bosses get out of your revenge?"

"They reward a faithful servant and remove a fly from the ointment."

"It's nice to know I'm a fly at least."

"It pleases me that you keep your sense of humour, but no, you're not the fly. You are not special, not to the 'boss' as you call him. You have value to me, but it's your plan they want to remove."

"Easily done. I promise to be a good boy."

He laughed again.

"I'm going to miss you! I'm afraid it's not that simple. Besides, where's the fun in accepting your word. You are my link to finding Jesus, I know you are. Belial told you how to find the last demon and you are going to tell me what he said."

"Why would I do what you want?"

"I'm sure you don't want to, but you will. We've danced these steps before. You don't even need to tell me — I can simply pluck it from your memories."

Lazarus lied, I felt sure of it. If it were true then why didn't he just do that with the Friar and Hammond? He must have been torturing them for information, not for fun or to spur me into doing something stupid, although he'd succeeded on that front. I looked at the fallen holding me. They should have been able to do the same.

Something didn't seem right here.

"If you think you can, you're welcome to try."

He nodded.

"I think I'll soften you up first. Why make the task more difficult than it needs be? I'm sure that a man like you would taste very special. These two provided adequate starters, but now it's time for the main course."

He looked at each of the fallen, first one then the other. I braced myself to prepare for what was to come. When it did it slammed me from both sides.

Fire raced across my arm and across my body from the right. My skin blistered as the heat bit deep into my being. I cried out as the flames spread and a blast of cold from the left froze my flesh with sluggish ripples. Ice cracked along my arm and formed across my body, its bite no less severe than the flames.

Where the two met I experienced agony undreamt of. So far the afterlife had been an escalating lesson in suffering. What would come next? Now that thought was almost worse than the pain — almost. The cold and the fire raged and fought a war; my body provided the battleground for this elemental struggle. I screamed with all my will, a miniscule attempt to vent the agony which shredded every fibre of my being.

It stopped without warning and so great was the echo of my suffering that I didn't notice until Lazarus' face slowly resolved into focus.

"Did you like that?" he asked.

I struggled to find the strength to spit a clever comment back at him. Pride alone wouldn't suffice in this case. I spluttered, but with no conviction or coherence.

"Too much to speak? That's fine, I understand. Have another taste."

For variety they switched sides, fire from the left and ice from the right. The detached part of me remembered a story I'd been told by a junkie many years ago; he enjoyed injecting his drugs, but had an unusual method. He'd inject coke in one arm and heroin in the other. The two drugs have very different effects and they battled within him like two venomous snakes.

I wished I could swap places with him in that moment.

No such luck, of course; fresh pain seared my spirit and raged with the opposites. He let me scream for longer this time. The pain reached such a level that I feared my mind would fracture under the pressure.

The pain stopped again and I sagged between the two angels. Lazarus lifted my face so I could see him. His smile filled my blurred vision.

"I can tell you really enjoyed that one. The next one will be even better; in fact let's really spice it up. Unless ... Unless you'd like to tell me what you know?"

I summoned enough strength to shake my head.

"Modern day humans have such an interesting turn of phrase. For example, when two men are penetrating a woman from each end it is call a spit-roast. Even better, with three men it is called the Devil's Fork."

That didn't sound promising. I liked it even less as they bent me forward and gripped my ankles.

The duet of fire and ice formed again and then a third pain joined the mix. It travelled up my legs — no, that's not right — my legs sank into it. My body disintegrated from the pool of acid spread between his fingers. I howled, and even the detached part of me vanished under this assault from the triumvirate of pain.

My ability to resist dwindled. I would have to tell Lazarus what he wanted to hear.

No, there was another way.

A sanctuary within me.

I had been stupid; I could have escaped there at any time and with a thought I did.

And that was the mistake Lazarus had been waiting for.

Chapter 34
A Man's Mind is His Castle

Too late I realised that I'd played into Lazarus' plan. I sensed his assault the moment he launched it. I'd escaped the pain and that left me vulnerable; when I tried to return to normal time it was already too late. It hadn't occurred to me that the barrier which protected me while in normal phase disappeared when I slipped into my memory space.

When his presence penetrated my sanctuary I comprehended my mistake. He came in alone; the two fallen maintained their assault of fire and ice. The pain wouldn't reach me here, but it sapped my strength which reduced the reserves I'd need to fend off his attack.

As soon as I realised that he'd penetrated my defences I responded according to how the Friar had taught me. I also mixed in a little twist I'd learned from Lazarus; I thought he might enjoy the irony. I layered shields on top of each other, some smooth as I could make them, the way the Friar had instructed.

They slid into place more easily than when I'd been alive, and more importantly they bound so tightly that I couldn't detect any imperfections. I wrapped an alternating weave of moving threads between the smooth layers. Between the threads were the tiniest of gaps, a flaw in the defence. Lazarus would find it hard to focus on their continual movement.

I fortified the kernel of my consciousness with everything I had, confident I could maintain the barriers against his onslaught. My opinion changed the moment he struck my defences. They didn't even slow him down.

I restored the layers as quickly as he tore through them and his advance forced me to retreat so that I could maintain some distance from him. Though the delaying tactic bought me time, it also cost me considerable energy — energy I didn't have to spare. He appeared to have a boundless supply of it.

It didn't take a genius to realise that this wouldn't be a winning strategy. I needed to take the offensive. I knew full well that Lazarus outgunned me, so I had to find some advantage. Surprise usually provided a good leveller so I collapsed the multitude of shields into a single spear which I thrust into Lazarus as he surged at me.

For an all too brief second he looked surprised. I followed my attack, seeking to capitalise on this momentary advantage. With a swift movement he cut the lance of my will and absorbed it into himself. He shivered as he consumed my essence, and the expression of surprise melted into one of pleasure.

Never being one to learn a lesson easily, I charged and punched him in his smug smiling face. He laughed at my primitive assault, so I struck him again. He continued to laugh which irritated me more than my apparent inability to harm him.

I focused every fibre of my being into my next attack. I crashed against him with everything I had. I managed to rock him on his feet; every single piece of strength succeeded in disturbing his balance.

Impotent rage scoured my soul. No way would I allow this to be the end, not to Lazarus. Surprise had failed me. An all-out attack also failed. I needed something more imaginative. I stepped back and he opened his eyes, which sparkled with dark humour.

"Not giving up so soon, I hope," he taunted.

I had no intention of giving up, but I didn't want to waste my energy — especially as I'd realised that here in my memory I didn't recover my strength as well as I did in normal time. Lazarus had no intention of allowing me time to consider my options.

"Well this has been fun, and I promise you that we will have ample opportunity for you to enjoy more suffering. However, I do need the information you have hidden here in your memories."

Lazarus knelt and placed his palms against the ground. I sensed his will as it surged through my mind. As he did so I understood my mistake. When I died the transformation must have created the barrier which prevented casting out my will. It also worked the other way and prevented access to my mind.

I'd gained a new ability to return to previous moments and there the restriction vanished. What I didn't understand was how the barrier disappeared when I did so. I thought that it occurred only within my own mind. With the perfect vision of hindsight it made no sense and now I comprehended how I had opened myself to Lazarus' entry.

He'd made a mistake.

Normally when you enter a mind the mindscape is the person's mind; not so in this frozen memory. His will surged through the landscape, but he would never find the memory he sought, not that way. I realised his error moments before he did and it gave me an advantage to exploit.

The detached part of me had been busy thinking of a way to defeat Lazarus and it had formulated a plan. I created the memory, so the rules of its existence should be mine to command. If I left the moment it would collapse. I didn't know how that would affect Lazarus, but it had to be worth a shot. I needed to slow Lazarus enough to trap him so that he couldn't follow me.

I sensed Lazarus' confusion as he realised his mistake, and I summoned my tattered will into a tight ball. It grew hot as it condensed — within seconds so hot it glowed brighter than the sun. Lazarus opened his eyes and as he made eye contact I unleashed hell upon him.

He caught blaze immediately, though he didn't burn like a torch as I had recently. His flesh glowed as the energy coursed through him. He screamed as I had done. The sound filled me with joy.

The world around us collapsed as I slipped from it and into the next. Its existence ceased along with Lazarus and for a moment I enjoyed the satisfaction of defeating my enemy until a burning hand gripped my shoulder.

There before me stood Lazarus. A smile cracked his blackened face.

"A nice play; indeed, a valiant effort."

"How?"

"I too have learnt new tricks since passing. In some ways I should thank you for sending me across the veil and I will when we have time. For now I need the information Belial told you."

"I'm not telling you a thing."

"I wouldn't believe you if you did. No, we'll do this the old-fashioned way."

He grabbed me with his other hand. The burning had ceased and his skin restored to the original healthy hue. Fresh pain stabbed into me as his fingers lengthened and pierced my body. I cried out and struggled, the movement sparking further pain, yet still I resisted.

The pain destroyed my focus. I tried to escape but the moment collapsed; we returned to the Garden but Lazarus' will remained inside me. Then it simply became a matter of time. I battled for every second as he clawed through my memories, looking for the information he wanted.

Lazarus tore through my memories, delighting in what he found even though most was of little of worth. My resistance barely slowed him down. Within seconds he learnt that Belial had told us to seek Metatron in Heaven, although he didn't leave my mind until he had observed everything I had ever done.

Chapter 35
Not Part of the Plan

"I have it," Lazarus declared and withdrew his fingers from my body. The pain of his intrusion left me. I enjoyed the brief respite until I returned to full consciousness and the fire and ice took me again.

I have to say that I preferred the time when I caused pain rather than suffered it.

"Who do they seek?" Fire asked and released me. Ice did the same. The euphoria overwhelmed me and I drifted in a warmth so pleasant I never wanted to leave its embrace. The light warmed me — not the heat of the torture I so recently endured, but the gentle warmth of comfort.

A comfort I had not known since an early age.

I remembered her then: my mother, not with the bitterness of grief, but with the joy of love.

Love.

Love was an emotion I had never known since her death. I'd tasted other people's love when I entered their minds. I understood it enough to have known its power, to have created the illusion of it when I condemned their lives.

In all my adult life I had never experienced it for myself.

I recalled the fact with some sadness and a little shame.

Yet another change from the transformation to torment me.

My existence used to be so much simpler.

In life I had never known regret. I acted on impulse or by design — it didn't matter which — following the path I chose. I lacked balance and, looking back, I saw that.

What did it mean?

The transformation from life to my eternal soul travelled not only the path I had followed; it also wandered the paths I hadn't taken. In these paths I'd made different choices, some small, others more significant. In them I'd been a different person, a better person perhaps — but those reflections weren't me.

I understood the truth in that realisation, a fundamental comprehension of who I was. I also understood the failure of the transformation and indeed of God's plan. He wanted to understand humans, to glimpse the hidden workings of our minds. In doing so he did it in the same way he interacted with creation. He was everything so our minds too must be everything.

Humans are both simpler and more complicated than God assumed. We draw conclusions, blinker our thoughts, and channel them into the decisions we want — or fear, depending on our state of mind. At the moment of death everything experienced by the soul is measured, not only the fact of what was, but what might have been.

But that was not who we are.

Regret didn't form who I was, nor was it what I had turned into.

I thought of love and remembered my mother.

It constructed a pleasant illusion. I allowed myself to relax for a while, but my duty remained.

Duty presented an interesting concept.

Most people would describe it as making the right choice even when faced with an easier path.

Maybe I had turned soft in more ways than I realised.

In any case, Hammond and the Friar remained in Lazarus' control. His power was superior to mine by a margin even greater than when we first met. So I convinced myself that I wasn't doing the right thing by trying to save them. No, I wanted revenge and if that freed them then that was a happy by-product.

Flimsy reasoning, I will grant you.

Lazarus and the two angels had moved away and it sounded like an argument had started. I'd clearly spent longer in my pleasant little daze than I had expected. I lay on the ground, near where Hammond and the Friar were imprisoned in their pillars.

Hammond looked out of his prison, face a ruined mess and head slumped lifelessly onto his chest. To my surprise I hoped that he was still alive (or whatever you called it on this side of the veil). The Friar appeared more alert and he whispered, his words almost drowned out by the argument happening only a few yards away.

"You have to run."

He was right, of course. Lazarus and the angels had ignored me; they were too focused on their quarrel to take note. Or perhaps they'd assumed that I was too weak, too beaten to pose a threat, or even run.

"I can't, I have to get you two out of this."

I moved closer to him, careful not to make any noise. The Friar's voice was broken. When his lips moved I noticed that, although his tongue had mostly healed, it still looked misshapen and speaking sounded difficult for him.

"Don't be a fool. Your task is too important."

"Fuck that! You know that I can't do it without your help."

I actually meant those words. Even more surprisingly, I didn't feel any shame in admitting that I needed someone else's help.

"You can't beat them — they're too strong. Get out of here while you can."

"No, I can get you out of here."

I crept closer so I could reach him. I clambered to my knees and after checking that Lazarus and the angels were still occupied I pulled at the rock holding the Friar prisoner. It felt slick to the touch, like glass. I struggled to maintain a decent grip as I pulled at it.

Naturally it didn't move; it had fused into a solid mass. I poured my will into imagined muscles and strained until a despairing hiss escaped my mouth.

"Get out of here now."

"No! I will not leave you and Hammond."

"Now is not the time for you to develop a conscience."

"Don't worry, that's not going to happen."

I worried that might be the case.

"There isn't time for jokes. Get out of here. He needs us as leverage; he'll hurt us but won't kill us unless he has you."

He made sense; maybe I should get out of here. All the while I kept pulling against the rock, squeezing it so hard it cut my hand.

"And what do we have here?"

Of course it was Lazarus' voice. I'd left it too long.

"When we first met you were weak, but your will was strong. The transformation has messed you up — now you're soft as well as weak. Such a shame. Still, on the positive side it gives me another way to torment you."

One of the angels interrupted.

"Your game with this human is your own affair, but we must see our Lord immediately with the information you have learned."

It was difficult to tell them apart, but I think that was Ice speaking.

"No," Lazarus replied. "We have to continue the hunt. We have a lead, nothing more."

"That lead is only for a name, the name of one of the oldest angels in existence. An angel who has never left the very heart of Heaven."

"Challenging I agree, but we will find the Messiah and I will personally bring his head to our Master."

"Your colourful human epithets aside, that is a claim you cannot fulfil. We will return to Lucifer now. What you do with your new pets is up to you."

Lazarus looked me in the eye. He wore his familiar and so fucking annoying smile and he winked at me.

Chapter 36
Betrayal

In the same movement as his wink he reached out with both arms and speared both angels through their necks, or at least where their necks would be had they been human. I had to admire the balls on him; this was a bold move. The two fallen towered above him and radiated power. I knew from personal experience the strength he wielded, but to take on two angels ...

Well, the move surprised even me.

He'd told me that he'd learnt some new moves during his time here, and that did appear to be the case. Both of the fallen screeched. Their high-pitched cries drove me to my knees, and the Friar moaned in concert with their shrieks, although I barely heard his voice.

Despite the pain I couldn't take my eyes from the scene in front of me. Lazarus bellowed with the effort of his attack. I doubted I would be given a better opportunity. The question arose of whether I'd be better off facing the two fallen or Lazarus. Even though they had embarked on a war to eradicate humanity, they appeared to hold no personal grudge against me or the others.

It didn't seem that long ago that I wouldn't have been bothered by that.

Maybe if I waited for the right moment — when the fight ended, perhaps — I could engage the winner and hope they'd be sufficiently weakened so I would triumph. Relying on hope gave me pause. I'd never been a fan of hope, although in this instance some was better than none.

With no other plan available, I summoned my strength to be prepared for the right moment. In the meantime I watched the struggle between Lazarus and the two fallen. The fight ended much quicker than I expected. His arms deep in the chaotic mass of the fallen on either side of him, Lazarus' face showed the strain.

They writhed and contorted, twisting their forms to repel the invading limbs. Their keening cries reached a new pitch as he thrust his arms deeper. I kept waiting for the two fallen to retaliate, to unleash hell upon Lazarus. They didn't. The fight waged too deeply inside them, hidden by the complex dimensions of their physical shapes.

My own power boiled within me. I lacked the ability to release it so I'd have to launch a physical assault. With some concern I realised that, even if I could release it, the power inside of me paled in comparison to the titanic energies clashing between the three combatants.

Then the impossible happened.

Both of the fallen flared brightly for a brief second, and as the glow faded I saw their internal structures. Before there had been an impossible structure beyond my comprehension, which now solidified into something simpler. With louder shrieks the fallen were diminished.

A pulse travelled along Lazarus' arms and he howled in ecstatic agony as he consumed their power. Strong as Lazarus was, the energy he absorbed must have been enormous. I recalled the old man in the shrieker's domain who had been exquisite beyond belief.

The first victory proved to be the tipping point and now wave upon wave of the fallen's essence fired along Lazarus' arms to be absorbed into his own form. Within seconds the fallen had been reduced so much that they had almost vanished from sight.

Now came my time to act!

I threw myself forward and lanced out with spears of hardened flesh. The dense cloud of points struck Lazarus as he swallowed the final remnants of the fallen. As I touched him I felt the glorious heat of his skin and heard the exultation in his voice, the only sound now in the Garden's expanse.

My plan had little chance when I'd thought of it, but as soon as I touched Lazarus it went from a small hope to none at all. He'd assimilated the power of the fallen much faster than I'd anticipated.

He cast me aside with a tiny shift in his balance. I landed hard, but jumped back to my feet. Once again he seriously outmatched me, but I didn't intend to go down without a fight.

Lazarus held up his hand, indicating a truce. His face wore a beatific smile — the smile of a dope fiend after a hit.

"Hold."

I did as he instructed. It seemed like I had done so before hearing his command, and that worried me. Had he become so powerful?

"I don't want to kill you, not yet."

I didn't like the sound of that either.

"Why not?"

"Because we'll have so much fun together."

I doubted the 'we' part of his statement.

"Besides, I have an important task for you."

"Why would I do anything for you?"

"Because I have your friends."

"They're not my friends. You need better leverage than that."

"Nice try, but you forget that I've been inside your head; I know what they mean to you. As I said before, you're not only weak — you've grown soft as well."

"Don't listen to him! Get out of here now."

I looked over at the Friar; so did Lazarus, who pointed at the Friar and held his hand over his face. The Friar shouted in anger, then screamed. The screams soon ceased and when Lazarus removed his hand I saw that the Friar's face had been fused shut. His head bobbed frantically as he screamed his horror, but no sound came from him.

"That's much better; three's a crowd don't you think?"

"You bastard." I lunged at him and he caught me easily, tossing me to the ground again.

"Calm down. If you do as you're told then everyone will remain mostly unharmed. For now, at any rate."

"You really want me to help you out on the promise of more 'fun' when I'm done?"

"When you put it that way it is a hard sell. However, it does give you time and time gives you hope — no matter how slim — that you can find a way out of this. You won't, of course, but I am looking forward to finding out what you'll come up with."

"What is it you want me to do?"

"Ah, down to business. That's what I like to hear. I don't want anything from you which you weren't going to do anyway."

The Friar continued to thrash. I also noticed that Hammond had regained consciousness, although he was careful not to move. I'm not sure what he thought he'd gain from that. The volcanic rock held him secure, so he could hardly leap into action with a surprise attack.

I didn't reply and waited for Lazarus to continue.

A few seconds passed. He smiled his terrible grin and nodded.

"Ok then. I want you to continue your quest for the Messiah."

"We're not looking for Jesus."

"Are you so certain? I know this is where your quest will lead you, but you will need to find out what Metatron knows. You will then come back to me and tell me what you have learned."

"That's crazy. How am I supposed to get to Heaven with all the shit happening? I doubt I'll find my way there."

"I can get you to Heaven. From there you'll have to figure the rest out for yourself."

"I have no idea what I'm doing!"

"You do yourself a disservice; you're a resourceful chap and I'm sure you will find a way."

"I don't know anything about Heaven. I couldn't even recognise Metatron in a crowd."

An idea occurred to me.

"If I had help then the task would be easier."

"What help?"

"The Friar and Hammond have got me this far. They have the knowledge I need."

I didn't know whether they did or not, of course, but if I could get them out of Lazarus' clutches then we'd have more room to manoeuvre.

"I don't think so — after all, who would keep me company while you were gone?"

I had no answer for his question and apparently he didn't expect one.

"Are you really going to make me threaten your friends?"

"Why don't you track him down yourself?" I thought that playing on his pride might help in some way. "You're stronger than I am. You just took out two angels without breaking a sweat."

"Yes I did. However that won't help me there. No, I am not welcome in Heaven. They would detect me the moment I enter."

"Won't they realise I've entered Heaven as well?"

"Maybe, but that's your problem, not mine."

Wonderful.

"So what will you do if I find that the last true demon is in Heaven?"

"That remains to be seen."

"Especially as it looks like you've burnt your bridges with the other side. They're going to be looking for you."

"It's unfortunate, but also none of your concern. You have only one thing to worry about and that is finding Metatron and discovering what he knows."

I remained silent once more, waiting to see where he would go next. Lazarus didn't appear to appreciate my stalling tactic.

"All right, you want to do it the hard way? That's fine with me."

He strode to where Hammond hung slumped, still pretending to be unconscious.

"Your friend Hammond can stop his little pretence. Now — one last chance to take the easy path. No? Never mind."

He placed his hands upon Hammond's chest. His fingers lengthened and burrowed into Hammond's flesh, dividing to form a web that spread under his skin. I'd seen something similar before; this reminded me of how the Antichrist had ripped the miracle from my body. I didn't want Hammond to experience that agony.

"Ok, I'll do it."

Lazarus shook his head.

"It's too late for that now."

The web now covered all of Hammond's body and with a mighty wrench Lazarus pulled all of the flesh from his frame. Hammond's scream filled the sky. Lazarus shredded the lumps of his essence and consumed the tatters with evident relish.

Hammond's body remembered what it should be on the inside, but not so much that it stopped him screaming despite the lack of vocal chords. His scream tore through me. I could no longer hide the fact that I did indeed care for this man. Yes he'd imprisoned me, a few times in fact, but he was a good man.

Scratch that. Being a good man wasn't what I liked about him. No, he'd always been a man true to himself, no matter what life threw at him.

The scream stopped as Lazarus tore Hammond's remains into shreds and swallowed them. He smiled at me with a scrap of Hammond's flesh dangling from his lips, then delicately wiped it away.

"That's better. Now we can talk."

Chapter 37
Knocking on Heaven's Door

The pillar holding the Friar burst into flame and he screamed. I rushed to him. The scorching heat slowed my approach, but I didn't let it stop me. I tried to smother the flames with my body, warping it to cover the Friar. These were no normal flames and they continued to burn.

My skin blackened from the flames and I howled in concert with the Friar. Without warning Lazarus dragged me from the Friar and cast me to the ground.

"As much as I'd like to watch you burn, you have work to do. Don't worry, the fire won't kill him; he'll soon wish it did, but he'll keep burning."

"Stop! I'll do what you want, just stop the fire."

As petty as it sounds to me now, those words hurt to say. The detached part of me didn't care — it remained happy to say whatever needed to be said to free myself from the situation. It hadn't suggested I agree and then leave the Friar to his fate, but I'm sure it would at some stage. What did surprise me was that I argued with this sensible aspect.

"Yes you will, but the fire continues and will keep burning your God-bothering friend until you return with what I seek."

"You can't!"

"You can plainly see that I have. Now shall we get started, or would you like to watch your friend burn for a bit longer? He has a fine screaming voice, don't you think?"

"I'm going to ..."

"Yes, yes I'm sure you'll try. Now, are you ready?"

I wasn't, but what choice did I have? I simply nodded my acceptance.

"Good. Now I'm happy to say that this is going to hurt you a lot."

"What do you mean?"

"I'm sure you know that humans can't travel in the same way that angels can, but like all laws there are ways round it. I have found a way. Unfortunately for you this won't be a pleasant experience."

"Well let's get on with it."

Lazarus placed his hands upon my shoulders and the world snapped.

I no longer heard the Friar's screaming and I counted that as a blessing.

My form stretched. No — stretched implies a gradual process. I exploded. The cloud of my being filled creation for only the briefest instant and he'd been right, it hurt.

There's probably some irony in the fact that I'd experienced greater pain since I stopped torturing random strangers than I ever did before.

The flood of sensory input was even greater than the shattering pain. I filled creation, and for the same moment it filled me. I saw, heard, touched, and smelled everything that existed and it proved too much for my mind to process.

Density is the amount of matter within a volume; the larger the mass the greater the density, and so too with the smaller the volume. Within the smallest moment I held the greatest possible amount of information and it hurt.

Infinity.

Or as close as damn it.

I wanted to scream in fractured horror, but I feared that extra piece of information added to my mind would be enough to break it. My mind had grasped many things since the transition, new concepts and new values and now this.

The moment froze and I learned everything. I saw the Garden in its ruined glory, the bloodied mud from millennia of war now buried under the guts of the Earth. Armies of angels marched across the cooling lava.

With all the events I'd experienced recently the eternal war had become a remote concern, but here I saw it waged in all its might. Hell remained empty except for the few watchers, set there by Lucifer in case others tried to infiltrate his realm like we had.

Lucifer marched with his army — a vast host spread across the southern borders of the Garden. His army was dwarfed by the struggle to the north, but it still looked formidable. The fallen jostled and wrestled with each other, vying to consume the most souls. They'd started with the humans within their own ranks, although not all were devoured. Some, like Lazarus, had proven their worth, or were strong enough to survive.

In the initial feast they harvested most of the billions of souls scattered around Eden, the freshly dead from our world's demise. They gorged upon these stricken souls and grew fat on their essence.

A fierce battle raged along the border between Eden and Heaven to the north. The loyalist angels held firm against the massed forces of humanity, the human souls who had banded together over the previous centuries.

The moment slipped into the past and I coalesced back into my limited form. The great pain faded and with it my understanding of the wider world. The loss of that knowledge filled me with sadness. I remembered parts, but not the details. The infinite complexity of a single angel seemed but a grain of sand compared to what had filled my mind and I mourned the absence of comprehension.

The horror lasted for only a second. My mind snapped back to its normal frame of reference quickly, the cold part providing the much-needed anchor. I looked up and realised where I stood. Lazarus had kept his word and I now faced Heaven. He'd placed me on the other side, far away from the battle lines.

Heaven presented a sight of such splendour it caused silent tears to stream down my face. It had been so long since I cried that

I didn't realise at first. It felt strange, but also a good feeling. Here I stood in the presence of something so great I understood the meaning of humility.

Not for long, but for those few minutes I surrendered myself to awe.

Technically Heaven refers to everything in creation, but it most often refers to the city (for want of a better term) of the loyalists. Unlike Hell, the city of Heaven was a place of synchronicity and cohesion.

Hell had also been a place of wonder, but it had been a confusion of artistic glory from a multitude of genius minds. Heaven formed a single piece of art from gifted artists all working in unison.

Vast structures of intricate patterns towered above me. I saw designs within the structures and followed them with my focus. They curved inside themselves in ways my mind couldn't fathom. All of my stargazing hadn't prepared me for the mathematical majesty I beheld here.

Perfect order.

That was what Heaven represented.

Chapter 38
God's Champion

Somewhere inside this maze of crystalline perfection I would find Metatron. I didn't know how I would locate him, but I would do it. The vision of the Friar as an eternal flame flickered in the forefront of my mind.

As could be expected, Heaven's form was completely different to the more individual and open feel of Hell. And it was far from deserted; even from the outskirts I detected angels patrolling the structure. The city appeared to be formed into a single architecture. No signs of individuality identified one part from another.

The sight stunned me and I would have happily stared at this marvel forever, but the Friar's continual torment forced me to hurry my actions. I first had to find Metatron, and in that task Heaven's form provided its assistance. Although Heaven presented a cohesive whole something did stand out.

A tower stood at the centre.

I deduced that this tower, this single sign of something different, had to be a clue — at least it provided me with a destination, somewhere to start my search. Its position at what I guessed to be the centre of Heaven also indicated some importance, perhaps a proximity to God.

Thin reasoning I'll admit, although it did give me a place to start.

The next problem I needed to solve was getting to the tower. I guessed the guardian angels wouldn't appreciate me simply walking in. I didn't know how carefully the angels watched, but I doubted the guardians were there simply for show.

I recalled the shriekers' domain and how I had blended with the fabric of their realm. I also thought about the tunnels we had created after escaping Belial's tower. I could use the same technique to sneak into Heaven.

Belial had created a tower. While it didn't look like the one I wanted to reach I wondered if there was some connection.

I lay on the ground and the warmth seeped into my back. It felt pleasant, comfortable, and secure — for the moment. I relaxed, banishing the image of the burning Friar to the deep recesses of my mind where the cold part took over the vigil.

When I blended with the shrieker domain it had been easy, almost instinctive. The same had been true for the tunnels under Eden. Here I didn't slip into the fabric; the structure appeared different, more complex. I sank a little into the ground, but encountered resistance. A square peg in a round hole, I didn't fit the geometries used to create this realm.

That made some sort of sense to me; the domain had been created by human minds. God had created Eden specifically for humans so he must have changed the structure to make it easier for humans to manipulate.

What about the tunnels under Hell? My cold part raised a valid question. While I didn't have the answer it did indicate that I should be able to blend, unless Heaven had a different structure to Hell. I told that part of me to be silent.

Maybe some of the fallen had made it easier for the humans to form the tunnels under their domain.

Sometimes I wished this new remote part of me kept its thoughts to itself.

Perhaps loyal angels did the opposite with the structure of Heaven to prevent humans from altering its form. After all, Michael believed that humans didn't deserve to become part of Heaven. Lucifer seemed to be more pragmatic. He only turned against humanity once they posed a threat to him.

That might have been an interesting thought, but it certainly wasn't a useful one.

I told the distant part of me to keep to itself unless it had a useful suggestion. It didn't, so remained quiet for the moment. I returned my focus to the task at hand.

My will remained limited by the confines of my body, but in this instance it proved to be a boon rather than a hindrance. I probed at my skin, pushing it into the surface I rested against. Since my transformation from living human to an eternal soul I'd made the same mistake we all did. We brought the baggage of our bodies with us.

Humans are biological creatures, slaves to our evolution. This is natural; after all we were physical creatures. Our brains developed into one of the most complex structures in the known universe and from this incredible biological machine we gained our minds.

Like our brains, the mind is an amazing thing, but at the heart of it all it is sparked from meat — clever meat, but meat nonetheless. The soul was created by God to capture our minds and expose how they worked as part of his grand thought experiment.

The problem we faced — or in a more immediate sense the problem I faced — was that bodily encumbrance. Sure we'd developed tricks to stretch that dependence, yet it still lurked deep inside, limiting our capabilities. The constraint on our potential stemmed from the form we relied upon, not just on the surface, but the mess of organs beneath the skin.

When I probed inside my body those organs did not exist, but I did sense the ghosts of them. The problem was more fundamental than that. We came from a physical universe, one with a very different structure to this level of reality. The physical world was composed mainly from the repulsion of matter — volumes of empty space between stars, between galaxies, even between atoms.

Here everything formed a much denser structure where matter was not organised by the space between things. Instead of the space in between dimensions coiled tightly, they stacked upon each other in ways that created infinite possibilities.

I didn't need to comprehend the complexity straight away. Like any good human I possessed a talent for simplifying problems. In human terms I could blend into the fabric of the domain because the structure had been made less complicated. In a sense it provided the space I needed to merge.

No such allowance had been made in Heaven's form, so I had to find another way. I remembered the Friar's teachings when he'd first revealed the truth about the gifts I possessed. He had taught me to search for the tiny gaps which existed in all things; on the face of it, useless advice in my current situation.

Not so useless upon reflection, though.

The kernel of what he'd taught was not to blunder straight into a problem. Instead I should examine it from every angle. I could unravel this secret and I didn't need to understand it to achieve my goal.

I would find a way in.

I pushed and poked from the inside, using the construct I imagined as my skin to explore the surface of Heaven. I found no gaps, but that was all right — it simply confirmed what I had thought.

Next I took sections of my skin and rolled them into each other. I collapsed the volume I inhabited into myself. Bit by bit I made myself smaller, repeating this with the rest of my body until I reached maximum density. It didn't seem much smaller than when I started. You have to start somewhere, though.

The next stage proved a lot more challenging. I folded a small piece of my body within itself. I didn't merely compress it into a smaller volume — I twisted it into a new space, in effect creating a new dimension. The reason it proved so difficult was because the relic of my human brain didn't like thinking of more than three spatial dimensions, so I cheated. I parcelled up the three I had, flattened it and extruded it at right angles from the three existing ones.

To my surprise it worked — not at first, of course, but after a few attempts I managed to hold the structure long enough for it to slide into place.

I did it again.

The process worked more easily this time, although it required more focus than before.

I did it again.

And again.

I kept repeating the process until I discovered that I'd sunk deeper into the ground. Not by much, but enough to know that I was on the right track. I twisted and extruded over and over again, changing my form to become a plane, the size of a napkin and just as flat.

Increasing the complexity of my component dimension not only reduced my physical size; it also improved my compatibility with Heaven's structures. It had taken far longer than I'd hoped, but I could finally infiltrate Heaven in what I hoped would be a covert fashion.

My increased integration with Heaven's fabric conferred another advantage: I gained a new sense. I'd worried that my condensed form would dull my senses, but that didn't seem to be the case. I could now also sense the locations of angels if they were close to me.

In other words I knew where the angels were.

Yes, it was confusing.

I rolled with it. I needed a break and now I had one. I didn't intend to poke this gift horse in the eye so I headed in. At first I thought that I would have a better chance of moving undetected by travelling inside Heaven's fabric, but that proved to be a bad idea, as I should have known. The interior became even more complex than the outside.

It also lacked anything resembling the normal layout I would have assumed for a building. I sensed no passages or rooms, only an endlessly evolving fractal pattern which led me in impossible directions.

I decided to retreat to the outer surface. It would be a more practical route and so I slid along the ornate decoration of Heaven's façade. The tower looked a very long way away.

To my surprise, the trek to the tower proved uneventful. After all the build-up I avoided the angelic guardians relatively easily and I caught some glorious views of Heaven's architecture along the way. I didn't rush. The last thing I needed was an encounter with one of the angels. After my dealings with Lazarus I doubted I would be any more successful against them.

As I approached the tower I noticed something strange about it. It looked very plain compared to the rest of Heaven's magnificence. When I moved even closer I realised something even more bizarre. It wasn't so much the lack of decoration, but the simplicity of it.

I didn't see any of the recursive patterns or structure beneath its surface.

An odd puzzle indeed.

I stopped to survey the spectacle around me and drink in the view when I reached the base of the tower. While I didn't know for sure, I sensed that Metatron lurked somewhere close to hand. It may have been instinct or some other sense, perhaps even self-delusion, but I knew that my search drew to an end. All I needed to do was enter the tower.

Nothing is ever as simple as it should be.

I sensed them in the instant before they appeared; the split second warning didn't help me at all.

Four angels appeared at each cardinal point around me.

One looked immeasurably brighter than the others — as bright, in fact, as Lucifer had been when I'd seen him in Belial's chamber. The density and complexity of his form rivalled that of Heaven itself. I realised who this was, this being of such power that it hurt to look at his glory.

"You do not need to hide. Your journey has reached its conclusion."

The Archangel Michael's voice resonated with a timbre that compelled me to obey him. Of course, I hesitated. No matter how powerful the foe, I would never show the fear which now gnawed in the pit of what was once my stomach.

"Come now; it is easier if you come with us."

Still I hesitated. Two of the angels reached into Heaven's skin and yanked me from my deluded hiding.

"You always did enjoy doing things the hard way. Well, that's fine — we're happy to accommodate you."

With those words everything turned white.

Chapter 39
The White Room

For a moment I thought I had passed out and become lost in a dream. In time I would wish that I had. Featureless white surrounded me, a pure bright light filling my vision in every direction. A hollow silence pressed against my mind, urgent in its embrace. This didn't seem like a dream, though. The reality presenting itself here contrasted with my more usual (and usually a lot more entertaining) dreamscapes.

Understanding came to me in stages.

My senses, or rather the lack of them, provided my first clue.

I saw nothing, only the white. I assumed it to be light until I looked down at where my body should have been and saw nothing at all. That didn't seem so bad. I was quite familiar with messing inside other people's heads, so being a disembodied entity didn't strike me as so frightening.

So too with touch. I lacked a body, so having no sensation of touch wasn't too strange. The lack of anything else around me did seem a bit peculiar. I assumed that whatever existed there would be revealed in due course.

I've never been the most patient of people, but I could be when circumstances forced me to. It didn't mean I had to like it; still, I rolled with it for the time being.

The lack of a sense of smell didn't worry me at first. The same applied to taste. I detected nothing there to trigger those senses.

The silence didn't concern me either, not immediately. That precious delusion lasted until I called out to demand what the fuck was going on.

I didn't hear my own voice. Now that was unusual.

When I invaded people's minds the reality of their inner space became pliable to my will. Even when the person possessed enough will to resist me, some impact of my presence could be detected.

That didn't happen here.

I tried to move, but movement requires some frame of reference, and I had none. I detected no change in position, no sense of movement — nothing to indicate that I had moved at all.

I called out again and heard nothing.

Then panic set in. I smothered the surge with my will, but beneath my conscious mind it lurked, ready for release.

There was no option but to wait. I couldn't even sit or lie down to wait in comfort. I possessed no body, no form, and no senses — only thought in an endless sea of white.

Time passed and stretched into an eternity. I counted the moments to pass the time, but I soon found that it didn't help. Signifying the passing seconds with my counting only made the moments take longer. In truth it didn't really matter how long I had to wait; I had no other option.

The end of the waiting came when I heard a voice.

No, that didn't seem right. I heard nothing. The silence wasn't simply an absence of noise; it had become the definition of my new reality. The voice wasn't a mere voice at all: it represented the sudden understanding of words from an unknown source. With no sound I detected no inflection or tone to help identify the source. It might as well have been a typed message.

Actually, that would have been preferable. At least I'd have had something to look at.

YOU ARE NOTHING.

A bold statement that clearly wasn't true. I existed here, wherever here might be. Even stranger, here might not be a place at all! I thought, I remembered, even if I no longer had any external stimuli to place me in any known reality.

Where am I?

YOU ARE NOWHERE.

I am somewhere. Where have you put me?

TO BE SOMEWHERE YOU MUST BE SOMETHING.

I think, I feel, I am.

THOUGHTS ARE NOT REAL.

My thoughts are real.

They were all I had in that moment, a being of no substance but with thoughts, memories and purpose.

YOU HAVE MEMORIES?

Yes, I remember.

WHAT DO YOU REMEMBER?

Everything, I remember everything.

ONLY GOD CAN REMEMBER EVERYTHING. ARE YOU GOD?

No.

OF COURSE NOT; YOU ARE NOTHING.

I am me!

WHAT IS YOUR PURPOSE?

Only then did I understand the game. This was a simple interrogation, admittedly in an unusual form.

My purpose is my own.

YOU HAVE NO PURPOSE BECAUSE YOU ARE NOTHING.

And so it continued, on and on. The questions repeated in an endless loop. The cadence changed, but never the ceaseless search to learn my purpose.

Over and over, the same questions, the continual denials of my existence — and eventually I slipped. Not so much that I revealed my purpose, but enough for a tired and stray thought of the existence of the last true demon and the key he provided to slip through.

My quest to find some way to undo what had been done and restore humanity's existence. I caught the thought before it formed and in that moment I comprehended the beauty of the method.

By denying my existence, it forced me to think about who and what I was. I only had to think to reveal the information my tormentor wanted. That definitely made the game harder to play. Try it yourself — you mustn't think of the murder you just witnessed and everyone around you is talking about.

It's not impossible, but it does take some doing.

Pride might have been my greatest sin, or at least the root of all of my other sins, but it was also my anchor. The anchor proved to be what I needed to keep my focus away from revealing my purpose in Heaven.

It wasn't easy, though.

The ordeal continued for an age. So long in fact my distraction technique started to crumble. The feeling of smug satisfaction also faded.

The constant bombardment from the voice that wasn't really a voice.

Anger proved to be the first crack in my armour.

To put it simply, the voice pissed me off.

I challenged it and cursed it. I realised it had to be an angel, but it presented no personality that I could attack. My curses were vague and, despite the rage which fuelled them, they failed to satisfy or dull my anger.

I might as well have been punching at smoke. It made me tired and I failed to inflict any damage. The anger weakened my resolve and once again I almost slipped and revealed what I shouldn't.

My next tactic was inspired by a clip from a documentary I'd once seen while stoned and watching TV. I remembered a grizzled Special Forces veteran describing their interrogation resistance training. He'd stated that the moment you communicated with your interrogator you had lost. It wasn't advice easily used in my current situation. Figuring out how I could turn it to my advantage gave me something new to focus on.

I tried ignoring the questions instead of responding to them. I kept my mind blank, although I've never been into meditation so I found that very difficult to maintain. My interrogator appeared to understand my new tactic, so the pace of the questions changed. My mind would blank and as I slipped into the routine of nothing another question or statement designed to shake my fragile poise slammed into me and stirred my thoughts.

Mental fatigue hampered my efforts. The questions were repeated so many times that it became difficult to maintain focus. I held on by playing a word association game in reverse. Whenever a question pounded its way into my mind I reflected the demand by thinking of the opposite. The ploy worked for a while, until the questions changed and became less direct.

This subtler attempt proved more difficult to counter, especially as I'd become so weary I struggled to concentrate. I so desperately needed to rest. The assault intensified, no longer a cat and mouse game. Instead the words bombarded my mind with vicious blows. In a panic I switched to a new tactic: I sang songs in my head.

I'd always had a good memory, not just for the lyrics of songs, but the music and even the voice. I clutched at those memories and used them as a shield against the relentless attack. I repeated the same songs over and over again, forcing myself to produce the perfect renditions and getting angry at myself when I faltered or made a mistake.

The presence responded by increasing the ferocity and rhythm of the questioning. Words blurred in my head faster than any of the guitar riffs I played to counter the intrusions. It worked for a while, and then my attention slipped again.

THE DEMON? YOU KNOW WHAT THEY ARE.

I swore at my mistake. I was so tired.

Then it struck me; I cursed myself for not thinking of it earlier.

I slipped into my memories, seeking a frozen moment. I found respite and I fell into its warmth.

THERE IS NO ESCAPE.

Damn it!

The questioning resumed, now focusing on the last true demon — what did I know about him and where did I expect to find him? I responded using the techniques the Friar had taught me. I weaved a shield around my mind hoping to block the invading questions. No barrier that I constructed made any difference.

It mocked my weakness.

Anger lent me strength although I took care not to surrender to it. Its presence failed to stop the interrogation.

Without warning the questioning ceased.

I didn't understand why. In fact, my will was so shredded I feared I might reveal my purpose at any moment. I welcomed the silence, which provided me with the respite I needed. Sleep beckoned me with its siren call and I so wanted to collapse into her arms.

With no eyes to close I willed my mind to shut down. I was so tired I didn't understand why I didn't pass out.

The silence expanded, dwarfing me with its immensity. It swallowed my hope as I realised that sleep wouldn't come to comfort my damaged psyche. It stretched on and before I knew it I was lost to eternity.

Chapter 40
Unexpected Visitor

Nothing lasts forever. There is always a beginning and an end.

Lost in the silence, it might have seemed like forever, but it did end. The chime of a bell broke the silence. In normal circumstances the sound would have been so delicate I probably wouldn't have noticed it. In the gaunt quiet it rang louder than a gunshot.

Before me stood an angel. He appeared magnificent. His face was ageless and his eyes reflected deep wisdom. He wore a familiar form, which was of the classically rendered angel with alabaster skin, a perfect physique and a face more beautiful than the one which launched a thousand ships.

Some aspect seemed familiar about this angel; I felt sure that I'd seen him somewhere before.

"Who are you?" I asked him. My tone was harsh only because I hadn't spoken in what seemed like centuries. "Holy shit!" I exclaimed as I realised I could hear my own voice. You cannot imagine how amazing it felt.

The angel glanced around. I wondered what he was looking for in the white emptiness and I guessed that he shouldn't be here. Now that piqued my interest.

"Who are you?" I repeated.

"I am the one you seek."

His voice murmured whisper-quiet, as faint as the bell that tolled his arrival, yet I heard it clearly.

"I am the Metatron."

"How do I know that's true?"

"The fact that I shouldn't be here should be enough."

"Well it isn't — and where the fuck is this anyway?"

A nagging question lurked behind my apparent rage. I didn't have a clear picture of it; my thoughts remained confused. It also occurred to me that this might be a trick, another attempt to force me to reveal my purpose.

"This is the void."

"I don't understand what you mean."

"It's a place where Michael imprisons those who betray us."

"So why am I here?"

"I don't know, and that's why I'm here. Michael hates humans, so much so that he has worked to destroy them entirely. Yet here you are and your presence makes me curious."

"How do I know you are who you say you are?"

"You don't. If you were an angel I could prove the truth to you. As you are human, you'll have to trust me."

"Why should I do that?"

"If I wanted to harm you there's nothing you could do to stop me."

"You're just another part of their questioning."

"Wait; they were interrogating you? What did they want to know?"

I pondered whether or not I should tell him, although if he was helping them then it didn't matter — he would already know. If he wasn't then I had nothing to lose anyway, or did I?

My brain had been stretched so thin I couldn't think properly. I had to take a chance.

"They wanted me to tell them why I am in Heaven."

"And why are you in Heaven?"

Here went nothing.

"I'm looking for you."

"Why are you looking for me?"

"I need to find the last true demon and I was told that you might know where he is."

Metatron leaned towards me. I saw an odd expression flit across his face.

"And who told you to seek me in this search?"

Amidst the confusion, a moment of clarity — and with it understanding blossomed.

"You sent me."

I knew I was right, but I didn't understand how that could be. The collapse of Belial's domain must have meant that Lucifer had killed him. How was it possible that he now stood in front of me?

More puzzling was how I'd known. The knowledge had been revealed in a flash of understanding. Belial and Metatron where the same being.

"I didn't."

"You did, I know it was you. You are Belial."

I saw understanding in his face.

"I am not Belial."

"You are."

"I assure you I am not, but I understand why you'd believe so."

"Well, feel free to share."

"Before I tell you that, I need to know why you are looking for the last true demon."

"I need his help to contact God."

It sounded so ridiculous when I said it out loud. I believed in the quest and, just as importantly, I wanted it to be true. I caused the destruction of humanity. Ok, I didn't do it, but my failure had enabled Lucifer's plan and that didn't sit well with me. I've never been a fan of losing.

My old friend pride! They say it goes before a fall, and my pride had preceded the biggest fall in history. I had to make it right and any chance, no matter how slim, would do. I also trusted the Friar's judgement and he'd followed the plan.

The vision of him burning in the rock with only Lazarus as company filled me with anger. Anger and pride — a volatile combination and my cup certainly overflowed.

Metatron watched me in silence. I guessed that he weighed what I'd told him. Now he needed to decide whether to trust me or not.

"I hate to be the one to tell you this, but your plan wouldn't have worked."

That really wasn't what I wanted to hear.

"What do you mean? Hemal seemed so sure."

"Hemal? The name is familiar; yes, she is one of Michael's angels, although I can't imagine why she would think that the last demon would be able to help you."

"Why are you so certain that it wouldn't work?"

"Because it has already been tried."

That wasn't the answer I expected.

"What do you mean?"

"There were never very many of us; after the purge only three remained. After watching the evolution of your race, and then the actions of the angels in conscripting you into their war, one of us decided to intervene."

"Wait, what exactly are you?"

"Well, with Belial now destroyed I suppose I am the last true demon. That's what the fallen call us. The loyalists just call us abominations and they are forbidden to speak of us.

"As to what we are ... Well that's a little complicated."

"Try me. Everything appears to be complicated these days."

He nodded.

"Agreed, nothing is ever as simple as it should be.

"We came into being at the same time as the one you call God. Nothing that exists should be alone. Even he finally realised that truth and it's what caused him to create the angels."

"Wait, what are you saying? That you are a god?"

"With the singular presence which is creation I know why that would seem presumptuous, even to one such as you."

I'm not sure what he meant by his last comment, but it didn't matter for the moment.

"We all came into being at the same time. I believe we were intended to be equals, that together we provided the seed for creation. Something happened in the instant at the beginning of it all. I've never known what it was, and I guess we may never know. That something caused one of us to be stronger than the others and he became creation and the rest of us just tiny unknowns within his body."

I thought of cancer and he frowned at me.

"Can you read my thoughts?" I demanded.

"I'm aware of practically everything which exists. My brother might dominate creation, but we siblings still form part of the original spark."

"So why can't you communicate with him?"

"I don't know. We've tried throughout the history of creation, but we have never succeeded. The last one who tried believed that God knows we exists but chooses to ignore us."

"That doesn't make sense. Why would he ignore you?"

"Again, we don't know — and when Jesus went to find out we never saw him again."

I didn't like that revelation. I didn't like the fact that Lazarus was right.

"Where did he go?"

"He tried to intervene, to represent humanity to God and to try and end the war and humanity's place in it."

"I take it he didn't succeed."

Metatron shook his head, his face sombre.

"He tried repeatedly to commune with God, to communicate directly, without any success. After much debate he decided that to truly represent humanity he needed to become human. Only by living a human life and becoming a soul upon death would he truly be a part of creation and then be able to communicate with God."

"I don't understand. Aren't you part of creation already?"

"In a sense we are; we existed when it all began. However we aren't part of Heaven."

"I thought Heaven included all of creation."

"Not quite. He created Heaven and it occupies almost all of creation, but not the entirety of it. We are the only parts that aren't, although it's only me now."

"I'm sorry. I wish I could have helped Belial."

"I saw from your memories that you were there, but trust me, there was nothing you could have done. You are very strong for one of your kind, but you are no match for the forces arrayed against you."

I really didn't like the sound of that.

"How could Jesus become human? I've been told that angels cannot transform — that they could only possess humans."

"That is true. Angels are of Heaven, even those who have fallen."

"So how did he manage it?"

"It wasn't easy and if your universe had been part of Heaven then it would have been impossible. Even so, it took all of his essence to create a single cell in the womb of the woman who would become his mother."

So the virgin birth was true, then. After all I'd learned it didn't surprise me.

"He lived his life and returned as a soul. We watched and were horrified by the things which happened to him. Your people can be very evil when confronted by what they don't understand."

I nodded, although I recognised all too well that evil wasn't only inspired by fear. Sometimes it was a life choice.

"He had changed when he returned, but he was still determined to communicate with God. Michael learned of his arrival in Eden and hunted him down. When he found Jesus he saw that Jesus wept — he wept tears of anguish because all the tribulations he had suffered had been for nothing. He still failed to contact God.

"Such was his despair that he didn't resist when Michael destroyed him."

"Why didn't any of the others realise this had happened?"

"We did, Belial and I. Michael didn't want his followers to know that the purge had not been completely successful. There were rumours of the last true demon, me, which he couldn't erase. It seemed angels liked to gossip as much as humans."

"So what do I do now?"

"I don't know. Perhaps you can succeed where we failed, but you have to find a different path. I can get you out of here. After then you need to leave Heaven. If Michael finds you after you've escaped he'll destroy you."

Chapter 41
Failure

"Why would I do that? This insect is nothing to me. His kind are no more."

I recognised Michael's voice immediately, as did Metatron.

Metatron stepped in front of me, blocking my sight of Michael. The bright white light around us dissolved and we returned to Heaven, appearing at the base of the tower I had tried to infiltrate. It might not have been appropriate in the circumstances, but I still couldn't help but marvel at the rich complexity of the architecture around us.

The first thing I noticed struck me as odd: Michael stood alone. I recalled what Metatron had told me. Michael had destroyed Jesus alone. Why would Michael be so secretive about killing his enemy?

"Ah, Metatron — I should have known you were the last remaining abomination."

Michael moved to one side. He kept his true form of constantly shifting fractal patterns which pained my eyes to look at. Despite that pain my sight was drawn to him. He looked like the detailed fabric of Heaven itself, which made sense I guessed as angels were formed from the same material as Heaven.

Again I sensed that there was a clue there, a truth so obvious that I failed to see it.

Metatron moved to counter Michael, once again blocking my sight of him.

"You're very protective of these creatures, Metatron. You always have been. What are they to you, I wonder?"

Metatron remained silent, although he made sure to keep himself between Michael and me.

"Nothing to say? I'm surprised. The Voice of God silent. I never would have imagined such a thing was possible. Truly this is a day of wonders."

A wonder indeed. I decided to enter the conversation.

"How was this possible?"

Michael looked at me. Metatron moved too slowly to block his gaze and I discovered why he had taken the trouble to keep between us. I realised then that he'd been toying with me before; there was no way I could hide anything from this archangel. His gaze scorched my entire being, penetrated every moment of my existence.

"You have some spirit for a lesser being, and I did enjoy your attempt as resistance. There was no reason for it, of course. If I wanted information from you I would have simply plucked it from your mind."

"So why?"

"You already know why. I see the comprehension making itself known inside you. I needed you to draw out this abomination; I'd long suspected, but in the tower he was safe."

"What is special about the tower?"

"The tower is of no concern to you. The fact that you think your words have some power, some hold to bend me to your will amuses me. We will talk, if only for a short while. You deserve some small reward for your efforts."

"What do you mean?"

"You'll discover that soon enough. Now be silent. There is a more important matter that I must complete."

I attempted to respond; nothing clever, just a show of defiance, but I couldn't speak. Or move, as I discovered a moment later. I would be a spectator for the main event.

"If you destroy me you can never undo your action," Metatron said.

"Your kind should never have existed."

"That isn't your choice to make."

"It appears that it is."

"Why?"

"You should never have been. I'm rectifying the mistake."

"We are not a mistake, but killing me would be."

"You can bleat all you like, but the fact remains that you are not part of creation, so creation doesn't need you. More importantly, God does not need you polluting his existence."

"I say again, how can you be sure? Has he told you that?"

"The truth does not need to be told."

"I existed long before you, Michael. Surely there is truth for you there?"

"Yet you are not part of creation."

"You're right and that's a mistake we can fix, but not if you destroy me."

"The only mistake is that you exist at all. Now we have talked enough. I have a war to win."

"Wait!"

I heard the pleading in Metatron's voice. Up until now he'd maintained a calm demeanour. Michael appreciated the change in tone, but it didn't save Metatron. Michael paused only to smile at his defeated foe before launching himself at the last true demon.

How did I comprehend that? Michael didn't wear a human form; the configuration of his shape changed as it did constantly. Maybe there was a pattern there which some part of me deciphered. Or more likely I simply imprinted what I could understand onto something which I didn't.

Michael attacked in a savage fury, the ecstasy of the kill written clear on his face. He tore Metatron apart and the demon didn't even attempt to defend himself. He screamed, though — a horrendous sound signifying the torment of the archangel's assault.

When I heard the world die it had filled me with horror. This sound from Metatron managed to sound even worse. This represented something more profound, something deeper even than the end of my world.

It was obvious that Michael could have ended it quickly. Metatron offered no resistance. He didn't even try to fight. I poured my will into my limbs in a vain attempt to intervene; Michael sensed my effort and paused his attack for a brief second, long enough to cast a grin of vicious delight in my direction.

That struck me as odd. The look of sheer joy at the destruction he wreaked on Metatron seemed so human. I wondered if I had imprinted my own assumptions onto his behaviour for the second time in as many minutes.

Michael's voice, though — that I didn't imagine. The words indicated there was something personal at work here.

I gave up on my attempt to move, and Michael took this as a sign to continue his attack. This time the attack appeared slower, more deliberate. The form didn't change, though. He tore quivering chunks from Metatron but didn't consume them. Instead he reduced them to dust and let them fall to floor where they dissolved into nothing.

The screams finally ceased when the last piece of Metatron disappeared into a wisp of vapour. The last true demon was no more.

Michael turned his attention to me.

Rage bellowed from my mouth. He'd released the control he'd placed on me. I could now move and stepped towards him, but a tendril of his being snaked out and held me in place.

Another puzzle: why had he restrained me physically when he'd already locked me in place with his will?

So many questions and very few answers. In that regard Michael did provide some balance.

"Now creation is free from that abomination there is only your kind to dispose of. And a war to win, of course — a victory too long a time in coming."

"You've lost the war, Michael," I told him.

"There will be no more of your kind. Heaven will no longer be plagued by the ever-increasing swarm of beings that do not deserve to exist in the same realm as God."

"You've still lost."

"Why would you think that? Ah, of course; Lucifer's plan."

He issued a complicated and musical sound that I guessed was a laugh.

"It was a good plan, but obvious that Lucifer would try to swing the agreement in his favour."

I couldn't disagree with that.

"So you did the same?"

"So obvious that even you understand."

I knew he'd tell me; I thought I even understood why. Michael the great leader, God's champion, had somehow outsmarted Lucifer. Unfortunately that wasn't how the story should have ended. He had to defeat Lucifer openly, but the direction this conversation headed indicated a sly ploy, not one of open combat.

Michael was smart enough to know that to maintain his authority he had to play his role, but he wanted to show off. He felt proud of outsmarting his great enemy and, to be honest, I wanted to hear how he'd managed it as well. He'd tell me because I was nothing, destined for oblivion.

That last thought didn't sit well with me. Still, what other choice had I but to listen?

"His ploy was obvious. With the sudden demise of your kind he had to try and claim all those souls for himself. The possibility of doing the same did occur to me. Unfortunately Lucifer's followers were more ingrained in your world than mine."

"What do you mean? I don't understand"

"Of course you don't, but don't worry, I'll explain it for you."

Most gracious of him.

"Lucifer had been proactive in establishing his followers on your world; he always had a purpose for you. If it had been up to me then we would have simply destroyed you like the abominations that came before."

"Why didn't you?"

The energies which comprised his being flared, an indication that maybe I should keep my questions to myself. Still, I expected him to kill me when he'd finished anyway so I didn't really have anything to lose.

The silence stretched and I wondered if he would answer my question. Eventually his form calmed and he spoke again.

"The fabric of your universe was beyond my direct reach. I tried with everything I had. I tried to grip the deceptively simple structures which formed your universe but I couldn't cross the threshold."

"So how did you pull our world from the universe?"

"Lucifer and I came up with the same plan, although we each did so independently. We established believers across your world. Together with possessed humans they formed a web that we could use like a net to pull your home into our own realm."

"But Lucifer had more sway than you?"

"Curse that traitor! Why couldn't he follow God's plan like the rest of us? Why did he have to follow his own path?"

"Maybe that was God's plan?"

That really rattled his cage.

"You dare! God's plan is perfection. It is the transforming of creation into Heaven's splendour."

"And then what?"

"There is no then, only the everlasting quest for perfection."

I wanted to ask why such a quest was needed. Surely God had already achieved perfection? However, I also wanted to hear how he had outsmarted Lucifer. A slim hope existed that I could use the information in some way. How I didn't know.

If only I could escape from Michael.

"Ok, so you both set up a network of minions which enabled you to drag Earth into Heaven. I don't see how that gave you an advantage over Lucifer. His army has already consumed the influx of souls. They have feasted and now march towards Heaven."

Again I heard the same complex, musical sound.

"You have been away from events for some time and many things have passed. I expected Lucifer to feast upon the souls which passed into Eden. My followers weren't strong enough to bring the world through on their own. They were, however, quite capable of a different task."

As Michael bragged of his plan, the calculating part of me called me a retard for not realising how I could escape. I took the berating like a man, careful not to the let my thoughts show — which was difficult, as I knew that Michael had the ability to pluck my thoughts at will. I hoped that he fixated so much on his own cleverness that it didn't occur to him to check what I plotted.

"The timing had to be perfect and my followers didn't fail me. At the moment the world was removed from your universe the mechanism which controls the souls' transition was modified. I'd looked for a flaw in the mechanism since its creation and discovered that only during the state of transition was any manipulation possible."

"Wait, you altered God's method for transforming souls?"

Why did I say that? I now had a plan; I only needed the information and then I was gone. I didn't need to provoke him, but old habits die hard and thankfully Michael ignored my question.

"I don't like taking risks, but I had to take this one. Lucifer could have detected the change in the souls easily. I calculated that he wouldn't and that his greed would override any caution and he and his forces would consume the fresh souls quickly so that my forces couldn't.

"Naturally he did as I expected and he and his minions gorged upon the recently dead. Two birds with one stone I believe is the human saying."

"What did the change do?"

"The closest parallel from your world would be a virus. The structure of the soul replicates and destroys angelic dimensional strings, the forms which bind our energy."

"In other words you poisoned his food source."

I was impressed — the so-called Father of Lies tricked on a huge scale.

"Exactly. And, combined with a peace treaty with the rebel humans on Eden's border, Lucifer and his army were weakened and attacked by the human forces. It was a glorious battle. The coward Lucifer ran, the humans took many casualties and my own army is currently busy cleansing creation of the survivors.

"Soon Heaven will exist only for those who deserve it. God will be served by my loyal servants, the way it should be. And you have no place here."

I took the hint. It was time for me to leave.

Chapter 42
Cast Out

The calm part of me deep inside reminded me that I could escape inward. I followed its advice — or at least I thought I did. Everything seemed to go as I expected. I slipped inside my memories and locked into a frozen moment. My plan had been simple; after my experience with Lazarus I hadn't expected the frozen moments to be safe, but I'd developed something new.

My plan involved skipping from moment to moment. I'd make the pattern as unpredictable as possible. I'd only spend the briefest instant in each memory before moving to the next. I hoped I would keep ahead of Michael as he followed me. I also hoped that I'd find a path in the memories that would allow me to escape his grasp.

No such luck.

I'd completed three jumps when Michael stopped my escape. He filled the moment with his presence. His energy overwhelmed my will. I still tried another slip, but it didn't work; I no longer possessed mastery over my own mind.

This didn't resemble the struggle with Lazarus. Then I'd been overmatched but still felt like I had a fighting chance. Against Michael I suffered no such delusion; his dominance was clear.

"I have not known any human to be able to do what you've just done."

I heard curiosity in his voice, and I wondered what that would mean.

"I had intended to destroy you as I did the last of the abominations. I see another possibility now, a greater entertainment. Lucifer's army is in retreat; most of your kind are dead, truly dead. The few who survive are anomalies like yourself.

"I wonder who will be the last — the greatest of you to survive this final trial. Maybe I would keep that lone survivor as a pet, as a memory of your failed species."

"I thought you wanted to annihilate us?"

"I do, but with only one there is no threat."

"So why kill Metatron?"

"They had power, you have little; not enough to threaten me or Heaven. Only in your ignorant multitudes did you pose any danger to the glory of Heaven."

I didn't like the idea of being anyone's pet, especially this archangel. I did, however, appreciate the idea of surviving for a bit longer. I still believed that I would find a solution for this mess, the pride in me certain I could fix what greater beings had broken.

"Yes, I think this will be a fun entertainment," he told me.

"Why would I play your game?"

"Because you think that time will bring you the opportunity you need to restore your world. You won't succeed, but you must try; a curious obligation considering how little you care for others of your kind.

"You would have failed anyway. God does not know that you exist, which proves that you and all of your kind were a mistake, an aberration who should never have been."

"I notice that you weren't confident enough in your belief to let me try."

"So try, speak to God and see if he responds."

I actually tried. I focused my will and here in my frozen moment I wasn't trapped within the limits of my body. I shouted with all my might, broadcasting my inner voice throughout Heaven.

I received no reply.

"I told you before that you were nothing."

I am not nothing.

"Yes you are — an imagining which animates itself, an insignificance barely deserving of the term."

I launched myself at him. I stood no chance of winning, but I was determined to go out fighting. A futile effort of course; He caught my attack easily and restrained me.

"So eager to die. Do you really not want to see the death of one of the few people you care about?"

I hadn't forgotten about the Friar. The cold part of me had hidden the memory to keep me focused. It had done so well. Not well enough to hide it from Michael, though.

"You creatures are such a conflict of contradictions; you lack purity of purpose. Well, not any more. Now you must survive."

The transition was smoother than when Lazarus transported me to Heaven, so much so that I didn't realise I'd moved until Lazarus tore me from my frozen moment back into Eden.

I glanced around; the scene looked different from when I'd left. The Friar appeared the same, screaming without pause as he danced inside the flames. His skin blistered and scorched, healed for a brief moment and then bubbled again as the flames bit deeper.

Lazarus, however, looked stronger. I dipped into the frozen moment again to look for clues. I saw him battle more of the Fallen as their retreat passed Lazarus' location. I saw him defeat one of the angels before he dragged me back.

As he stood before me I assumed that he had won the battle, which didn't bode well for me. He had been stronger than me before. Now his power had grown I stood even less of a chance. The Friar's screams chewed at my focus. Michael was right — he did mean something to me.

Unfortunately that fact didn't help. It limited my options and provided a distraction.

"Where have you been?" Lazarus demanded.

"I found Metatron as you instructed."

"And you decided to move in with him and play house with him for two weeks?"

"What?"

Two weeks! Had it really been so long?

"Where have you been? You left your friend here to suffer for a very long time."

"I was captured."

"Captured by whom?"

"Michael. He used me as bait."

"The archangel? He hates humans. Why did he let you live?"

"I don't know. He said it was for sport; he wanted to see what the last human would be like."

"That doesn't make sense, but neither does Lucifer's army dying for no apparent reason and in their thousands. And why they had to retreat from the border after sweeping through Eden."

"Michael tricked them."

"The day is full of surprises. It doesn't matter anyway. What did you find out from Metatron? Do you know who the last true demon is? Was it Jesus?"

He really wasn't going to like this.

"Metatron admitted to being the last demon. Michael used me as bait to lure him out. Belial was a demon too."

"And Jesus?"

"He was a demon as you thought, although it turned out that he wasn't the last of his kind. In any case Michael killed Jesus long ago."

"I knew it!"

Elation at being right, so quickly followed by disappointment with the realisation that revenge would no longer be his.

"You failed me."

"Wait! I did what you told me to."

"Yes you did, but you are no longer of any use to me."

Shoot the messenger.

The Friar suffered his wrath first. The flames flared in intensity, the cyclic healing ceased and his screams rose in pitch. I rushed towards him only to be driven back by the terrible heat. I watched him melt and his cries continued after his body no longer existed.

I howled in fury as a counterpoint to the Friar's fading shrieks of agony. No not fury. This was something more elemental that I hadn't felt since my youth: grief, bold and heavy. The cold part tried to disguise it as fury and it almost succeeded.

The Friar and Hammond: two people in the whole world with whom I'd formed a connection and now they were dead. Not merely passed on, but destroyed utterly. Lazarus would now kill me and that didn't seem like a bad thing in that moment.

Lazarus turned his attention in my direction and tendrils from him stabbed into me. Thousands of them needled into my skin and spread into a fine mesh. The Antichrist had done the same to me when he'd ripped the miracle from my being.

He paused for a second; long enough for anticipation to sink in. It didn't matter. I drowned in a sea of my own making. I howled, this time in agony. It made the waters turbulent, but didn't raise me above the surface.

Lazarus tore me apart layer by layer and I didn't care. Oblivion beckoned me with its siren call and I wanted nothing more. Waves of pain pushed me towards its shore. To feel nothing and to experience nothing had an allure that I'd felt on and off through all my years. Perhaps the time had come for me to finally surrender.

It was the greatest pain I had ever experienced and my mind barely felt it; but my body did, and I screamed with a vibrancy communicating the agony I suffered. The cold part did its job well and kept the pain at a distance, as if it was happening to someone else.

The memory of my body knew and it howled enough for all three of us.

I listened to that remote part of me, the part which had ruled my life before I died. It suggested that maybe it was time. I'd tried, no other options remained; there was no shame in giving up. There was nobody left to know.

That wasn't true.

I would know, and there was something which even the distant part of me couldn't silence — and that was my pride. I'd nearly given up once before and that had revealed a truth in the world I'd never imagined had existed.

If I gave up now what fresh opportunity would I miss?

The fate of humanity still rested on my shoulders. I didn't know how to lift that weight, but it felt good. It made me important.

The pain shivered through my body, but each wave was smaller than the one before as my form reduced with each layer torn away. I couldn't fight Lazarus, I lacked the strength to even slow him down and that was before he'd reduced me to living shreds.

Retreat, that was the only sensible option left to me.

Retreating inwards wasn't an option; Lazarus had already demonstrated his ability to enter even the frozen moments. Simply running wouldn't work either. A plan formed — probably not a very good plan, but what the hell.

I fell to the ground, which wasn't so hard. The pain I experienced meant that standing up hadn't been all that much fun anyway. Lazarus' monofilament fibres entered my body and I waited. The timing had to be just right.

He wrenched away another layer of my form and I used the wave of pain to energise the crucial step in my plan. As I rode the wave I focused all that remained of my will and sank into the ground. Eden eagerly accepted me and swallowed me whole. Lazarus roared with rage as I slipped from his grasp. He reached into the ground to prevent my escape.

I needed a single piece of luck for my plan to work. I hoped that, powerful as Lazarus was, he'd never had to change his form to pass through Eden.

Luck appeared to be with me as I sank deeper, Lazarus pushing tendrils into the ground to follow me. He encountered resistance the further he followed; it seemed as if Eden was trying its best to aid my escape. Looking back I wonder if that actually was the case, maybe even a sign? At the time I didn't notice but just kept moving deeper, transforming as I did so.

Chapter 43
That Familiar Café

I don't know how long I burrowed. I simply kept moving until I no longer sensed Lazarus' pursuit. For a while I drifted through the strata of Eden, allowing its presence to sustain and restore me until I felt recovered, although far from whole. I still felt lost. The decision to flee had been instinctual; without the pressure of the chase the imperative no longer provided any urgency.

With everything that had happened I needed to rest, to find time to plan my next move. My ultimate goal hadn't changed, but the urgency had lessened. As it ebbed my grief rose again, eager to reclaim its place.

The cold part of me hadn't given up; it realised that the only way to maintain some sort of equilibrium would be to keep me busy. I lacked the strength and the knowledge to go back into battle. I needed some space, so it directed me to somewhere I had found solace before.

Without realising my purpose, I constructed a domain of my own. When I'd stolen Lazarus' miracle the Friar and Hammond had bricked me up inside the wall of a monastery. It seemed so long ago, but probably wasn't. I hadn't been happy with that situation at the time and in truth it still rankled. I understood why they had done it, but it didn't mean I had to like the decision.

As well as feeling betrayed, I'd also discovered that the miracle came with a price. When Jesus had granted the miracle of resurrection and eternal life it had been intended for Lazarus only. When I absorbed the miracle it was like swallowing fire, a fire which burned in every part of my body without end.

Trapped inside the wall and tortured by the miracle's fire I had suffered for every single second. The only respite I found was retreating to the place deep inside me by the abyss. I had discovered the abyss during my days experimenting with the dark side of psychedelic drugs. I had revelled in taking people to the edge of the abyss and thrilled at staring into its turbulent depths.

I had built a Parisian café beside the abyss, less romantic than the Seine but it provided the refuge I needed. It did so again. This time the scene wasn't just a figment of my imagination; instead it became a domain like the others I had encountered in Eden.

I noticed differences, of course. The most obvious one was the abyss. The veil that separated life from death appeared above the café. Rather than a river beneath sheer black cliffs it formed the sky like a surreal painting. Unlike before when I existed on the other side of the abyss, I had passed through the veil and now only a few humans remained.

One of them was Lazarus.

At first that seemed like a big deal, but as time passed the pain of his memory faded.

The other change was that I became the domain, rather than wrapping an illusion around myself as I had before. It tormented me that I created such a wonderful place in which to hide — or rest — and I couldn't enjoy it. I remembered Hemal saying that humans couldn't be a domain and exist within it at the same time. Human souls sacrificed themselves to be the domain that others enjoyed.

That didn't work for me.

The remote part did its work well. I needed a focus, something to occupy my attention and here it was.

The puzzle wasn't an easy one to solve.

The basic problem boiled down to the fact that I couldn't be in two places at once. For a while and with a supreme effort I created a simulacrum of myself. I could even animate it, but it wasn't me. I tried my other idea and whenever I did the domain collapsed and I'd have to rebuild my sanctuary over again.

At times the frustration proved so much that I destroyed the domain. When I eventually calmed I'd rebuild it again and continue my investigation.

I decided there were two approaches to the problem. In the first I split myself in two, one part to be me and the other to form the domain. It sounded ludicrous but it was a possible solution. The other approach seemed more reasonable. I would have to find a way for a domain to become locked in place without my continued presence.

That must be how the angels had constructed Heaven and Hell, or so I assumed.

The real answer turned out to be so obvious I don't know why I didn't think of it sooner. I could escape in exactly the same way I had in the monastery wall. As to why I hadn't thought of it before, I had my suspicions — the part of me that wanted to keep me busy and didn't want me to use the easy route, although I wasn't sure why.

Unfortunately I would find out all too soon.

I delved into myself. Not into a frozen moment; that hadn't proved as helpful as it had at first, and besides, I didn't need to do anything outside of myself. I reconstructed the scene: the early twentieth century café, the ornate chairs and tables outside. The block pavement lined the front of the café and storm clouds boiled above the abyss.

In that moment I realised what the abyss represented. I already knew the abyss symbolised the veil separating life from death. I should have known all along what that meant. The clue came when it always appeared above the café and not along the front as it had before.

The abyss was immutable, a piece of reality completely separate from our perceptions. The wonderful thing about humans was that we held our reality within our heads — a subjective construct resembling the physical reality that existed around us, but malleable when we wished it to be.

I noticed that the abyss appeared to be immune to even my considerable ability to distort reality. I probed at it and sensed the familiar chill of its touch. It stretched when I applied pressure. I wondered what now lay on the other side. Up until then I had assumed that it presented a physical membrane dividing our physical universe from creation, although when I really thought about it that didn't make sense.

After all, why would this membrane exist at the centre of our minds?

The abyss was the process which connected us to our souls. It possessed no reality of its own, but its touch affected the reality around it. It was a process I believed couldn't be tampered with until my conversation with Michael.

If I could somehow force myself through the abyss would the process of my transformation reverse? Would I become what I had been before?

Those questions gave me some hope. If I could become what I was before, then ...

Then what? The thought seemed a pointless one. I remained limited in my abilities, but no weaker than before. The forces I faced were an order of magnitude greater than any I had fought back then. That poisonous seed quickly germinated.

For a time I concentrated on my private realm. I touched up the details and made it more real. I played house and became content for a while. It was an illusion, to be sure, but a comfortable one.

Comfortable, but lonely.

As before, I couldn't create companions. It didn't matter to start with; I'd been alone for many periods in my life. One aspect improved, though, and that was the food and drink. Before I'd only been able to create illusions. I had relied on Hemal and Venet (the bastard) to create refreshments which actually tasted real.

This time I was able to do the same and I indulged myself. I'd never really been one for enjoying food and drink for the sake of it when I had been alive. Now that I didn't need it, I developed a taste (if you'll forgive the pun) for it.

Fabulous dishes and rare wines caressed my palette; divine tastes distracted me for a time from my building depression. The transformation had changed me. It had instilled some human traits that I no longer had use for.

No, let me be truthful — it had awakened them. I wasn't born the monster I became. I developed into that through choice. Not a single big choice, but like many changes in life it had come in increments. Don't get me wrong. I didn't break down, and as with my own choices, the change didn't happen in a single switch.

These thoughts, these feelings, infected me slowly. Only when the ghosts of Hammond and the Friar visited me did I understand what transpired and by then it was too late.

They weren't really ghosts, I felt certain of that. They didn't come to torment me, although I often assumed they had. They were probably the creation of the remote part of me, the part which had kept me alive for so long. It realised that these new feelings confused me and kept me trapped in this cosy Parisian tableau. I imagined it thought that confronting the deaths which weighed upon my mind would provide closure.

Ultimately the approach failed, although things are rarely as simple or as obvious as they first seem.

They provided me with a form of company, at least; I conversed with them and we reminisced about the experiences we had shared. We talked and shared fine food until eventually we ran out of words. They remained, and became silent sentinels sitting at one of the tables. Occasionally Hammond revisited his role as waiter and brought us drinks.

I enjoyed the façade for a time, until gradually their presence became a bitter focus for the festering swamp at the bottom of my mind. Grief and disappointment in my repeated failures blended into a potent brew eating away at my sanity.

Too late, the sensible part of me realised what was unfolding — too many things repressed, too many feelings unknown but now rearing their fearsome heads. I couldn't battle these inner demons alone, and slowly they dragged me into the mire.

The Friar and Hammond remained, no longer created by the vengeful part who wanted to return to the fight, even if it meant losing. Instead they became manifestations of the foul mixture drowning my mind. It sounds simple and dramatic when I recount these events, but at the time it slipped unseen as a subtle poison, a death by a thousand cuts and I didn't feel a single one of them.

    I no longer dined upon the finest dishes. They provided no sustenance, but the drink proved a different matter. The dying parts of me welcomed this addition to their arsenal; imagined drinks shouldn't have caused intoxication, but they did and I revelled in it. I drank the fiery spirits, trying vainly to drown my sorrows, even though I felt that they would surely drown me first.

Chapter 44
The Fade

I sank slowly in a quicksand of my own creation, and I never even realised the threat it presented. All too quickly the insidious brew slipped over my mouth and I drowned. It happened so gently I didn't realise I was drowning. The brew tasted fine; self-pity was a luxury I so rarely indulged in and I made up for that.

Perversely it felt great; it didn't hurt, it bundled me in a cotton wool numbness which seemed greater than any joy I'd previously experienced. I didn't face pain, or torture or anything I could fight head on. The enemy had come in through the back door and I wasn't even aware.

The first step was a reversal of all the effort I had put into build my little tableau. I melted into the café and the surrounding scenery. I became one with everything, except the abyss gleaming with cold certainty in place of the sky.

When my merge with the scene became complete, it simply vanished and a fresh blue sky replaced the black membrane. Storm clouds gathered on the horizon. I smelled ozone in the air, but it didn't matter. When it rained the heavy drops splashed against brick, glass and stone, not the skin that once contained my essence.

Moment by moment I solidified into the domain. What had once been a figment of my imagination now became a construct within the fabric of Eden. The irony of all the effort I had expended — in truth, wasted — was lost on me.

The weight of my failures pulled me deeper, cementing me within my illusion made real. Hammond and the Friar sat at one of the tables outside the café. They drank black coffee but didn't speak. They didn't judge me; they didn't need to. Their presence was enough to remind me of their torment and my inability to save them.

I sank deeper in a vain attempt to escape the relentless horror of my guilt, a feeling I hadn't experienced for so long. They weren't the only visitors. Now that I no longer enjoyed the comforts of my dream it became more crowded than when I tried to populate the café.

An endless stream of people wandered along the street. Some I recognised; most I didn't. A few recognised the Friar or Hammond and greeted them as they passed. None of them stopped; they walked onwards, disappearing from view.

The weight of their footsteps pounded me deeper. I didn't want to see these people — the entire litany of my failures. I knew hardly any of their names but they had died because of my failure. I had overconfidently assumed I could destroy the Antichrist; it had even crossed my mind that perhaps he had power I might steal. Maybe something to dampen the pain.

I wanted to keep the miracle. Despite its fire, it had revealed my quest for oblivion to be a lie. Immortality stretched before me and I wanted to enjoy it.

My old friend pride had assured me that I would be able to defeat the Antichrist. I hadn't expected it to be easy. Defeating Lazarus hadn't been and then I'd had help. I did against the Antichrist as well, not that it mattered in the end.

One by one, then by tens, then in hundreds, thousands, millions.

Billions of the dead, all killed by my failure.

I despaired at the sound of their passing. They didn't speak. Their silence was eerie; all I heard was the march of their feet. They marched ever onward into oblivion, an end I witnessed as the Earth spilt its molten guts across the Garden.

Each footstep on my pavement pounded a nail into my being. This pain was unlike any other I had experienced. It wasn't a physical pain — the nails impacted on my spirit. I didn't want to endure this pain, I couldn't, and so like a coward I retreated.

Where were you when I needed you?

Deeper I sank. The café wasn't big enough for me to escape so I spread myself further, seeping into the fabric of Eden. I retreated and for a brief moment I found release.

For that short time I balanced on the equilibrium, but all too soon the balanced tipped and the weight of my guilt dragged me down.

The remote part of me didn't give up without a fight. It bombarded the overwhelming despair with logic. So what if I hadn't defeated the son of Lucifer? At least I had tried; I had battled and would continue to fight.

Except that I didn't.

His voice raged at me to wake up, to not slip away. Why had I escaped from Lazarus if just to allow myself to fade into nothing? That didn't seem so bad to me. The more I stretched, the more I thinned myself, the less the pain.

It didn't really lessen, but it did become more distant and that was enough.

I didn't want to hurt anymore.

So why not go out in a blaze of glory, or at least attempt to take Lazarus with me?

What if I won?

It should have been an uplifting thought, except that it wasn't. I really wish it had been. I'd always taken pride in my ability to control my thoughts and the scope they existed in. Now my thoughts were grains of dust cast in the air for all the effect they had.

They vanished into an overwhelming fugue of despair.

The remote part of me understood all too well what had happened and in truth I understood as well, but knowing a problem isn't the same as solving it. My will lacked any potency; as much as the two parts of me tried to keep the miasma at bay it was an elusive opponent that kept smothering me.

It kept dragging me down until I could sink no further.

As I sank I thinned myself out, but not with any real purpose — it was simply a consequence of moving. When I hit the bottom I spread my essence outwards. As I did so I discovered that I hadn't really hit the bottom. When I considered it the concept didn't make sense.

I discovered that the structure of Eden grew denser, more complicated, the form folding on itself in impossible geometries that hurt my head to even contemplate. Here lay a stratum more complex than anything I'd seen in Heaven, but in fairness I didn't try too hard to comprehend it. I didn't want to fight and I didn't want to solve a puzzle. All I wanted was to drift and become nothing.

An admirable goal (well, not really) and one that the fugue, which continued to coax me towards oblivion, agreed with. I stretched thinner and thinner. It seemed such a simple idea; my form diffused throughout the strata of Eden.

Some of my form touched the surface and continued to spread. In gossamer thin strands I flowed, yet somehow never quite becoming so diffuse that I ceased to exist. It all seemed too futile, and it occurred to me that maybe throwing myself at Lazarus would have been the better option after all.

That would have required effort, and seeping through creation required none. It felt more like a natural process than something I had to work at. I drifted and it wasn't unpleasant. The weight of my guilt spread across the vastness of my form and was lessened.

The borders of Heaven and Hell provided minor resistance, more like a bump I had to flow over to expand even further. Heaven shone beyond its former glory. I wouldn't have thought that possible. Or perhaps I now experienced it in a new way. I didn't perceive it with my senses — instead I filled it.

Its complexity had defeated my attempts to penetrate it before, but now I slid through the intersecting dimensions so easily it might have been guiding me along, aiding me in my development.

I passed through angels as my spirit travelled along the infinite paths. They didn't notice my presence. The atoms of my ever-diminishing existence swirled past the archangel himself and he didn't flinch.

It became obvious to me that the war was far from over. Michael's forces held the upper hand, but they couldn't press their advantage. The part of me filling Eden found the army of humanity. Only a few thousand of them remained.

However, these represented the finest and strongest specimens that humanity had to offer. They had retreated deep into Eden and stopped their pursuit of Lucifer's survivors. They in turn licked their wounds in Hell. Unlike Heaven, Hell had crumbled, the once glorious city now resembling a wasteland, although a few towers stood proud and strong.

Michael's deception had indeed decimated Lucifer's forces, but had not destroyed them and their leader remained a potent opponent. I wondered how the war would develop, but my curiosity soon faded, lost amidst the expanse of the being I had become.

I now filled Heaven, Eden and Hell. My form touched every living thing that remained in creation. Frustration shuddered through my person; I'd diminished but not ceased to be. A barrier blocked my final progression and beyond it I would end and be no more.

I seeped into the foundation of creation. I encountered no active resistance, but the sheer impossibility of it slowed my progress. I sensed that it was smaller than what I had already occupied, even the magnificence of Heaven. I encountered no active resistance, just pathways taking forever to follow.

Forever might have been an exaggeration.

The voice of my distant part quietened as I stretched myself beyond comprehension, but it made a final attempt to pull me from my glacial suicide. It shouted that there was a mystery here for me to solve.

I ignored it until the last fragment of my spirit filled this super dense crust of creation and the moment I did so I became nothing.

And I became everything.

Chapter 45
At One with Creation

In that moment I became everything that was and everything that had been. For the solitary instant I was everything and I was nothing. In that moment I had become so diffuse that it should have been impossible for me to think or feel anything.

Yet in doing so I became everything and I knew what it was to be God.

It proved too much. The totality of it overwhelmed me and I feared that my thoughts would explode. I had sought emptiness and oblivion — more than that, I had sought escape from my ultimate failure.

It's funny what life throws at you sometimes. For all my years, being in control had been the important focus and now I understood what it meant to be in control of everything. It was too much.

To slip into insanity would have been the sensible option at that point but as always I became my own worst enemy. I wanted to understand what it all meant and here was my opportunity to do so.

The moment passed and I discovered that I wasn't alone; another presence filled everything. It saw me and invaded me with its consciousness. It surged through me, not with violence but with absolute surety. For the briefest of moments I'd known everything. The knowledge faded, and in its place came an intelligence more complicated than the simple existence of things.

Only a second before, insanity had seemed a way out from the pain of everything trying to squeeze inside my insubstantial being. Insanity itself now seemed an impossibility. A voice drowned out my thoughts.

WHAT ARE YOU?

I remembered Michael's faked interrogation in the white reality, but that didn't even come close to this. Then the words had pounded into my mind like the ultimate hammer. This voice was so much more. It didn't intrude into my mind; it defined my thoughts.

There could be no escape from this will, but neither did I wish to defy it. From the moment the words filled my mind I knew what it was. This was the voice of God and his purpose focused in my direction.

You cannot imagine the completeness of it.

I pondered the question. There was no need to answer directly; my thoughts were his to do with whatever he wanted. I now remembered my life in quite a different way to the judgement of the Egyptian afterlife. I'd never done regret and I had no intention of starting; but still, the life I had led probably didn't sell my existence as a human being all that well.

YOU ARE A SELFISH AND BASE CREATURE.

I couldn't deny the accusation, but it irritated me to be told it all the same. It also annoyed me that the whole of humanity was being judged by my actions, that didn't seem fair.

WHAT IS FAIR?

Damn it, no privacy, even inside my own head.

I should have been used to that.

As for the question, it struck me as unusual, but I guessed that God only comprehended the rules which he defined. Fairness represented a human concept; admittedly the result of trying to make the rules apply equally, but still it meant that everyone should be treated the same.

Of course, being a human ideal it rarely lived up to its billing, but it did separate us from most of creation.

WHAT IS YOUR PURPOSE?

That familiar question, one I didn't have a clear answer for. I existed to make choices and simply to be; there was no grand purpose. I wondered about God's purpose. Why did he exist?

MY PURPOSE IS TO BE; TO MAKE CHOICES.

Interesting.

I calmed a little at this response. Even someone as cynical as me was a little overwhelmed at being in the direct presence of God. That's not to say that this presented a religious experience, or even a spiritual one. I did, however, comprehend a truth to the experience, a gravity that even I had to acknowledge.

In truth I experienced more than a little in awe.

WHY ARE YOU HERE?

Here was a simpler question to answer: I came here to save humanity. Well that wasn't quite true. I had given up at that point. My failure had led me to the promise of possibility. Another strange reflection of my life — great things came from adversity.

WHERE ARE YOU FROM?

I thought of the world, the blue orb in the majesty of space. I'd always loved gazing into the night sky. The majesty of it rivalled even the feeling of God's being inside my own: a sensation of the impossible, of the infinite within my grasp.

With some sadness I recalled the moment when the Earth had been ripped from the universe and dragged into Eden. Humanity had died in that moment.

WHAT IS HUMANITY?

On the face of it that was a simple answer to question: a race of people of which I represented just one. I detected confusion in God's demeanour which at first puzzled me. I remembered my conversation with Metatron and his revelation of what the demons were.

God was a singular being, not part of a collective like all other life forms in creation (actually that turned out to be incorrect, but isn't part of my tale). He created life, but it had never occurred to him that they should be alone. The confusion inside him deepened. For me the knowledge had been an interesting fact, but for him the effect appeared much more profound.

I AM ALONE.

And there it was. As humans go I wasn't the most social of people, but even I had never been totally alone. I still connected with others, even if they did become my victims. In some ways that provided far more intimate contact than even the most loving of relationships.

The truth boiled down to the fact that, while I was often alone, I was rarely lonely. Even when I occasionally felt that way it paled in comparison to God's loneliness. He knew no others of his kind and the last of them had been destroyed by Michael before my eyes.

MY KIND?

You were not meant to be alone; there were once others like you. I showed him the memories of Metatron.

HOW COULD I NOT KNOW OF THIS?

I had no answer for that. The angels had spoken of God not being aware of the demons' presence. Why that should be I couldn't guess. I did understand that God had allowed the destruction of my own people. It amused me to think of them as my people, but it was true. I was superior to them, certainly, although we were still of the same species.

Again I sensed his puzzlement.

I DO NOT KNOW YOUR PEOPLE.

You created them and now you deny them; somehow that seemed the wrong way round. I replayed my memories of the war in Eden and the destruction of humanity.

You created us as part of your experiment to understand choice. We make choices in the same way you do. We are like you.

NO.

Ah, denial. You allowed your creations free reign. Your angels conspired and destroyed your experiment. Did you create us purely for us to be their playthings?

In the hesitation before he responded I understood his confusion. He didn't see the angels as independent beings; he believed them to be expressions of his own thoughts. I comprehended his reasoning, and I also caught a glimpse of his mindscape.

God was everything.

I'd known that on an intellectual level, but I hadn't understood what it really meant. His mind was creation and he believed that he controlled everything in it. He didn't realise that the life forms inside him possessed their own wills.

And then I saw the horror of it.

I'd toyed with the thought of insanity; not knowing or being responsible had provided a momentary enticement. Inside God I witnessed something far beyond what I had imagined insanity to be like.

He represented reality, not removed from it or hidden by it; he was everything that could be. Since the first moment of his being he'd known a nagging feeling that something was missing. He didn't identify it — he couldn't — as he had no frame of reference for comparison.

The simple truth was that God was lonely. If there is no understanding that there might be something else, then how could you know what ails you? He didn't understand what the missing part of him might be, but instinctively he tried to remedy the problem.

His thoughts became angels.

Unknown to him, the angels interacted with God's brethren, whom they called demons, and in doing so gained their own free will. They developed and followed their own motivations. All the while God continued to believe that they remained his thoughts, but they didn't follow his will.

He didn't understand what happened to him. When they went to war with each other he feared that their conflict would tear him apart. He separated them and the war calmed for a while.

Why didn't you force them to your will?

THEY ARE ME.

Not any more.

Eventually the war resumed and the pain inside him grew, a continual torment without end. He created a sanctuary where he could escape, a universe of rules where his thoughts and will couldn't betray him. To his amazement beings appeared within this universe and they distracted the angels.

These new creatures fascinated God as well. They reminded him of the confusion in his own mind, yet how could such creatures exist in a reality governed by only a few simple laws? He wanted to understand these beings further and so created a way to transport their memories and experiences out of the universe when the beings died.

He had created souls.

I realised that God didn't appreciate the potential for the process he had created. He wanted to understand everything about humans, but that knowledge proved too complex. It could only be experienced by actually living their lives and so the souls replicated that purpose and human souls became alive when they entered creation.

The experiment wasn't a success to start with. The process drove many souls insane and infected God with more deranged beings. He created Eden as a memory of the world that they lived in, which worked for a while.

Humanity evolved over time, and the angels also showed greater interest in the arriving souls. God's mind was fragmented for time beyond measure.

The eternal question of why entered my own mind. What was God's purpose?

I AM.

There has to be more.

I MAKE CHOICES.

The kernel of something blossomed inside — an understanding so profound I didn't know where it came from. Metatron's face accompanied the revelation and I remembered his touch. I hadn't noticed it at the time. Presumably he had suppressed the memory, which had remained dormant until the right moment.

This moment.

Your purpose isn't just to be, it is to create.

I HAVE CREATED.

Yes, God was right; there had to be more to it than that.

Of course, the clue had been there from the beginning.

To exist wasn't enough. There had to be more.

I knew that the revelation was correct. God realised it too; I sensed his understanding. What lay beyond creation? Here humanity provided the answer: evolution. A truth some humans resisted, but it was there within us all the same.

Even God experienced the same motivation, the same unrelenting compulsion. We had to evolve beyond where we started from and develop into something new. Into what? That presented a fresh puzzle and no inspiration struck with the answer.

God's mind exceeded my own and he intuited the solution.

The answer was so simple it staggered me.

Chapter 46
Let There Be Light

A peaceful calm descended over me. God's presence remained, but he too experienced the peace washing throughout reality. I still felt stunned from the final revelation, the immensity of which stretched beyond even the vastness of God.

I am just a man; a powerful man to be sure, but God's presence had removed the blinkers from my eyes. I had deceived myself on many issues, all of them important to me but not important in the scheme of things.

WHAT IS IT YOU WANT?

I had a decision to make here. I had melded with God and now had a greater understanding of creation. I realised now that what I had originally set out to do wouldn't be possible, not in the way I had imagined.

I wanted humanity to live again, and to know that my last action wasn't one of failure. I'm a proud man, but not a vain one. I didn't care that no-one knew of my success. It only mattered that I knew.

IT CANNOT BE THE SAME.

Of course it couldn't.

I HAVE FAILED IN MY PURSPOSE.

True, but I didn't want to fail in mine. What had been broken could be fixed.

WHAT HAS BEEN CANNOT BE CHANGED.

That's exactly what I feared.

WHAT HAS BEEN CAN BE REBORN.

It took me a moment to understand the difference, but it sounded promising. Things wouldn't be what they were; the world would be reborn and things would be different.

YES, THEY WILL.

I thought about the revelation of God's purpose and, by association, our own. God's purpose is to create, not to control, but to allow the beings within him to develop until they too can create. So the great cycle continues.

I thought about the new world and wondered how it would be different.

Maybe I would be different.

I smiled; I didn't regret any of my choices. They might have been right, they might have been wrong, but they were mine to make.

Would I be different this time?

Probably not, but I looked forward to finding out.

LET THERE BE LIGHT ...

Thank you for reading The Last True Demon. I hope you enjoyed reading it. If you did then please leave a review or a rating on Goodreads, Amazon or wherever you share the books you read.

You can find out about my other books and keep up with my latest news on my blog:

http://thecultofme.blogspot.com